SISTERS IN ALL SEASONS

WINTER'S TIDE

We want to hear from you. Please send your comments about this book to us in care of zreview@zondervan.com. Thank you.

ZONDERKIDZ

Winter's Tide

Copyright © 2012 by Lisa Williams Kline

This title is also available as a Zondervan ebook.

Visit www.zondervan.com/ebooks

Requests for information should be addressed to:
Zonderkidz, 5300 Patterson Ave., SE, Grand Rapids, Michigan 49530

978-0-310-72619-7

Cover design: Kris Nelson
Interior design: Sarah Molegraaf
Editor: Kim Childress

Printed in the United States of America

12 13 14 15 16 17 18 19 20 /DCI/ 18 17 16 15 14 13 12 11 10 9 8 7 6 5 4 3 2 1

SISTERS IN ALL SEASONS

BOOK FOUR

WINTER'S TIDE

BY LISA WILLIAMS KLINE

ZONDER**kidz**

ZONDERVAN.com/
AUTHORTRACKER
follow your favorite authors

For Louise, Ann, Sydney, and Deb

1

DIANA

Two days before Christmas vacation, I was standing by my locker in the freshman hall getting out my world history book, which weighed about a hundred pounds, when I heard it. I'd been hearing it for a year now, and when it happened, I also always heard Dr. Shrink's voice in my head, saying, "Ignore it. Just ignore it," and always, up to this point, I had.

It was a girl from my gym class named Carla, and she was behind me saying, in a growly voice, "Annn-i-mal!" There was no real malice in her voice; it must have been something she was doing out of habit. A certain group of kids, the ones who wore designer clothes and wanted to make fun of the stuff I wore to the barn, who talked in loud voices about parties they'd only invited each other to, who stole their parents' liquor and talked about people behind their backs, called me "annn-i-mal."

And something in me snapped. A year of it, and I'd had enough. In a flash, I turned around and slung my book at Carla. The edge of the cover caught her on the cheekbone. She screamed and covered her cheek with her hand, and then she shoved me into the bank of lockers. My head bashed into my open locker door. A stabbing pain shot down my neck. The pain galvanized me, and I threw myself at her, knocking her to the floor.

As I got up on my knees, I heard a roaring in my ears that sounded like a freight train. People had started yelling, had started forming a circle around us.

And then someone roughly pulled me off Carla, and I was sitting in the hall, panting and crying, my heart pounding so hard I thought it might break my ribs.

A few minutes later the two of us were in Vice Principal Callahan's office. His red hair was mixed with gray, and he had a kind-looking face that belied the fact that he hated all of us and never showed a smidgen of mercy.

"As you know," he said, "we have zero tolerance at Bradley High for fighting. Anyone who fights is automatically suspended. No exceptions."

"I wasn't fighting!" Carla said, still holding her hand to her bruised and swollen cheek. "I was trying to defend myself. I mean, look what she did to me!"

"Why did you attack her, Diana?"

"She called me a name." The back of my head was throbbing from where it had collided with my locker door. I had put my hand back there but couldn't feel any blood.

"What name did she call you?"

"Animal."

"Is that true, Carla? Did you call Diana 'animal'?" Vice Principal Callahan's expression seemed to say he didn't think getting called "animal" was that bad compared to other things a person could be called.

Carla pretended to be shocked and innocent. "No! I didn't call her anything! I was just walking by, and she threw her book at me."

"Well, it's hard for me to believe that Diana would haul off and throw her book at you with no provocation. You're both suspended for five days. For the two days until Christmas vacation and again after school starts," said Mr. Callahan. "No exceptions. Call your parents. Now."

Mom's knuckles were white on the steering wheel as we drove out of the Bradley High parking lot. She had left work to come get me and was still wearing her white physician's-assistant coat.

"You say they've been calling you 'animal' for a year? Why didn't you tell me, Diana?"

"I told Dr. Shrink awhile ago. She said to ignore it." The only other person I'd talked to about it was Stephanie.

"And you ignored it until today. Why today?"

I didn't answer. I looked out the window. I hated it here. But I didn't know where I wanted to go other than the barn. I thought about grooming Commanche, about the way the warm air blew out of his nostrils, about the way his tail swished against his flank, and it calmed me down.

"Well, there is no appealing this," Mom said. "You were fighting. It's on your record now."

I glared at her. A thousand things I could have said raced through my brain, all having to do with how horrible it was to day after day go back to a school where people made fun of me. And it didn't really matter that those people were stupid and mean. At some point you have to fight back, don't you? Otherwise you get smaller and smaller until one day you disappear.

Once Mom got me home, she had to leave to go back to work. She said we would talk about everything later.

I wandered upstairs to my room, passing Stephanie's open door on my way down the hall. She had covered her bulletin board with pictures of herself and her friends. The latest pictures she'd put up were from our cruise last fall, with Stephanie and me and Lauren. The only thing I'd put on mine was a photo of me with Commanche.

I slammed the door, pushed the pile of dirty jeans onto the floor, and threw myself onto my bed. Mom was mad enough, but I was dreading Norm finding out what had happened. I knew that was why Mom wanted to talk later; she wanted to run everything by Norm. That wasn't the way it used to be. I felt like throwing a book at *him*. It would just prove to him, once again, that I'm a troublemaker. But I didn't care what he thought, right?

A few minutes after Stephanie got home from cheerleading, she came upstairs and knocked on my door. I didn't say, "Come in," but she peeked her head in anyway.

"Hi," she said. "I heard."

"Yeah? Everybody's talking about it?"

"I guess." She came in and sat at the foot of my bed. I was still lying there among the twisted covers. "What happened? What made you do it?"

"She called me 'annn-i-mal.' I just got sick of it. I couldn't take it anymore."

Stephanie looked uncomfortable and stared at the floor.

"Look," I said. "I know you think what I did is bad. But I'm not perfect like you."

"I'm not perfect!" she said. "What are you talking about?"

"You wouldn't have gotten into a fight with Carla. But I couldn't take it anymore, that's all."

"I'm not blaming you," she said. "People have been unbelievable about calling you that. I wish they would stop."

"I do too. You'd think they'd be tired of it by now."

"So you're suspended until after Christmas vacation?"

I nodded.

"I'll get your homework for you," she said, getting up and standing with her hand on the doorknob. She was wearing a T-shirt and those stretchy shorts they wore for cheerleading practice. Even though she'd been flipping around the gym for hours, her ponytail was still perfect.

"Don't bother. I'm not going to do it," I said.

"I'll get it anyway. You might change your mind."

When Norm got home, I could tell he already knew. Mom had probably texted him. I was up in my room and heard the garage door close, but I didn't hear the usual animated conversation that Mom and Norm have when they've been away from each other all day. Dinner was quiet, like there was a gigantic elephant on the middle of the table. And, sure enough, after Stephanie and I did the dishes, Mom and Norm said they wanted to talk to me but that Stephanie could go back upstairs.

I collapsed into the La-Z-Boy that Norm usually sits in because the two of them sat on the couch together, side by side, like they were on the same team or something. Which they were. Ganged up against me.

"We understand how frustrated you were today," Norm started out.

"Why do you always let him do the talking?" I said to Mom. "I'm not even his daughter, and he's making all these decisions about me."

Mom sat forward. "Diana, we are a family. We make decisions together. That's our agreement."

"Your agreement. Nobody asked me what I thought."

"We're on your side," Norm said. "You seem to be missing that, Diana. You're too busy being antagonistic."

I looked away. This was torture.

"This name-calling is a form of bullying, Diana," Mom said, "and we understand that. You were taunted and baited until you couldn't take it anymore. Yes, you threw your book at her, but you were provoked. And apparently they've been trying to provoke you for a year now. We're on your side, sweetie."

"But fighting isn't the answer," Norm added.

"Well, I guess ignoring it isn't the answer either!" I yelled. "What *is* the answer?"

"There is no good answer. The teachers and principal are aware of it, so that should help. They will be looking out for it," Norm said.

"We're going to ask to meet with the principal to appeal this being on your record. Meanwhile, let's discuss what this means. What should we do? Should we move you to another school?"

I ran my finger over a spot on my jeans. Mom apparently had done some thinking about the situation, because this sounded different from what she'd said earlier. She did sound more like she was on my side.

"No," I said. A whole new school would be scary. And it would be cowardly. I didn't want that. "I don't want to switch schools."

"All right," said Norm, leaning forward with his

elbows on his knees. "We'll fight back ... but not by fighting. How does that sound, Diana?"

I shrugged.

The next day I wasn't allowed to go to the barn, but there was an emergency appointment with Dr. Shrink.

> Dr. Shrink: Diana, why don't you tell me what happened.
>
> Me: I threw a book at a girl because she called me "animal."
>
> Dr. Shrink: You've been successful at ignoring it for such a long time. What happened?
>
> Me: I don't know. I just lost it.
>
> Dr. Shrink: Your coping techniques—counting to ten, taking deep breaths—seemed to be working so well. Nothing else going on?
>
> Me: No.

Not really the truth. There was a new guy in my Spanish class. His name was Noah, and he had long-ish, uncombed blond hair and had, so far, alternated between two different flannel shirts with his jeans. But he'd come up to me after class and asked me a question.

"Hey, what's the homework again?"

I gave him a look that said, *Are you stupid?* Why was he asking me? But then I told him. "The vocabulary on page eighty-five." Noah scribbled it down while I put on my backpack and started heading out of class. He followed me.

"Why do people call you 'animal'?"

I stopped and stared at him. He wore a small silver hoop in one ear.

"I don't know."

"That's kind of weird, don't you think?" Noah said.

"I hadn't thought about it." That was a lie. I thought about it all the time.

"I mean, it could be an insult. Or it could mean you're really tough. Like, a real animal. Which is it?"

"I don't know. I just know I don't like it."

We were out in the hall by now, and I turned left. He came with me.

"Why don't you just punch one of them?" Noah said.

I had had dreams of punching them. Dreams in which my fist connected with their chins in some otherworldly way and knocked them into the next solar system.

"I would," he said. And then he peeled off and went into the chemistry classroom, leaving me walking down the hall wondering what it would be like if I did punch one of them.

> Dr. Shrink: I think it's a good idea that your parents are going to talk to the administration.
> Me: It feels like I'm telling.

Dr. Shrink: You tried to handle it on your own, and that didn't work, so now it's a good idea to have someone on your side.

Me: It feels like I'm a baby. I didn't want to tell anyone. That's why I only told you. And Stephanie.

Dr. Shrink: How did Stephanie react?

Me: She's upset. She thinks it's terrible. She even offered to talk to some of the people she knows, but I said for her not to. I thought it might be bad to get help from her. It might make things worse. Or make things bad for her.

Dr. Shrink: I see. Normally it's best to try to handle these situations without making a big deal of them. But we all need support in our lives.

Me: Norm doesn't want to support me. He just thinks I'm a troublemaker.

Dr. Shrink: What makes you think that?

Me: (shrug)

Dr. Shrink: I bet that's not true. Remember, he jumped in the water and saved you when you fell out of the raft on your white-water rafting trip. He showed, by his actions, that he cares about you.

Me: I think his feelings about me have changed. I think the fighting thing made him mad at me. And also that I don't want to go to church. He wants the whole family to go to church and I said I wouldn't.

Dr. Shrink: Why does he want the whole family to go to church?

Me: I don't know! I guess he thinks it will help us "bond." (I hold up my fingers and do air quotes on the word *bond*.)

Dr. Shrink: And what about church don't you like?

Me: Everything. I don't believe in God. I think all those people sitting inside the church pretending to be so good are hypocrites. People do terrible things and then they go to church.

Dr. Shrink: And what about the people who do good things?

I didn't answer. I hadn't thought about that.

So I missed the last two days of school before Christmas break. Mom and Norm went to meet with the vice principal, and he said that because the school had a zero-tolerance policy for fighting, and I had started a fight, I couldn't be let off. All students must have equal treatment.

At this point Mom allowed me to go back to the barn. She dropped me off one afternoon while everybody else was still in school. It was a cold but sunny, sparkling winter day. I didn't have a lesson, but I planned to hang around and help Josie, the barn manager, with the hopes that maybe she'd let me ride Commanche.

I love the smell of the barn. I love the fresh smell of the hay and the earthy, living smell of the horses. Josie had put a Christmas wreath on the barn door and a small fake tree with horse ornaments stood on the desk in her office. She'd hung a stocking on each horse's stall door.

"I brought Commanche some carrots and horse cookies for Christmas," I told Josie. "Can I give him one now?"

Josie was sweeping the barn floor and wiped sweat from her temple with the back of her gloved hand. Josie is athletic and plainspoken, and she's always got horse hair and hay all over her shirt. "If you do a few chores around here, I'll let you ride later. How about that? And you can give him a treat then," she said.

"Yay! Thanks!" Josie was going to let me ride!

In fast motion, I mucked some stalls and filled some water buckets. When I finished, I stood outside Commanche's stall with the carrots I'd brought. With his peach-soft muzzle, he explored the flat of my hand and took a carrot in his teeth. I felt myself start to relax for the first time in three days. Why do I always feel like problems don't matter when I'm at the barn?

"Commanche was in a bad mood this morning, but it looks like you've perked him right up," Josie said to me.

"Can I ride him bareback today?" I asked. I figured she'd probably say no, but I wanted to ask anyway.

"No, it'll hurt his back," she said. "You know that."

"But I did ride bareback that one time when I had a lesson."

"That was when you were working on balance, and I wanted to make a point. The saddle is there for a purpose," she said.

But later she let me canter Commanche out in the ring. The cold air stung my nostrils, but I relaxed into the saddle and the rocking of Commanche's gait. It was perfect. Commanche liked the chilly weather and was frisky and cantered more easily than usual, tossing his head, vapor coming out of his nose. He's an old horse, about twenty or so, and sometimes he's lazy, but not today. I ran my palm down his neck.

"That's a good boy, Commanche. You're doing such a good job," I said. "The stuff that happened at school doesn't matter one bit, does it? Not one little bit. All that matters is you and me out here in the ring. Isn't that right, Commanche?"

One of his ears cocked back in my direction.

Afterward, while I was grooming Commanche, he made little snorts of pleasure and leaned up against me. I thought about that guy, Noah, from my Spanish class, telling me to punch someone, and I wondered if that had been on my mind and maybe that's why I'd done it.

On Christmas Eve, it was windy and cold. Late in the afternoon, as the sun was starting to set, Norm and Mom and Stephanie started getting ready to go to church.

I stood in the hallway outside my room, listening. I heard them all downstairs talking in the kitchen, the rapid click of Mom's heels, and the rattle of Norm's car keys.

"Colleen just texted me that they're sitting on the right-hand side, if we want to sit with them," Stephanie said. Colleen is Stephanie's friend from church, the one I don't trust.

"Oh, nice," Mom said.

"We better get going. Otherwise there won't be any seats at all," Norm said.

"Diana, we're going!" Mom called.

I came to the top of the stairs and looked down. Mom and Stephanie wore their red sweaters and scarves and gloves, and Norm wore his leather jacket. Mom's dangly Christmas earrings flashed a reflection of the lights from our tree when she looked up at me.

"Okay," I said.

"We'll be back in about an hour and a half," Norm said. "And when we get back, we'll open gifts with Stephanie, since she has to leave for her mom's tonight. If you need us, text your mom. She'll keep her phone on silent."

"Okay."

"Sure you don't want to come with us?" Mom said. "I bet you'd enjoy the Christmas carols."

I set my jaw. Back when we'd had the family meeting and Norm had suggested going to church, he'd said he wouldn't make us. "I'm sure."

"Okay, bye!"

The kitchen door to the garage closed behind her, and I heard her heels on the stairs. The car started. Car doors slammed. The sounds of the car engine receded as the car backed out and the garage door went down.

Then the house was silent and I was alone.

2

STEPHANIE

Even though we'd been to church without Diana before, I felt really bad about leaving her alone on Christmas Eve. Especially after what had happened at school. As we drove out of the neighborhood, past all the houses with Christmas lights just winking on, Daddy and Lynn talked about her.

"Maybe we should have made her come," Daddy said.

"Then she would just rebel and become resentful, so we can't do that, Norm," Lynn said.

"Do you think she'll ever change her mind?"

"Diana is very stubborn," said Lynn. "I guess we'll just have to give her time and see. Maybe she'll be an agnostic all her life. I was for many years."

"I didn't want to go to church for a long time after the divorce," Daddy said, "so I understand where she's coming from. She's going through a tough time. I just wish we could help her more."

I was used to hearing Daddy and Lynn talk about problems with Diana in front of me. Sometimes I felt jealous that they spent so much time thinking about her. I got the feeling that because I was an easier kid, they didn't focus on me as much because they didn't have to. But it was so much better than what was happening at Mama's house with my stepbrother, Matt. I had to go over there tonight and tomorrow for Christmas Day, and I was dreading it even though I missed Mama.

"So going to church with me last spring made you change your mind about God?" I asked Daddy.

"It did," Daddy said. "Just being there together with you, I suddenly had this feeling of peace. I saw how powerful God's love is and how it can transform our lives."

I sat back in my seat, warmed by Daddy's words.

Each of us was given a candle on our way into the

sanctuary. The Chrismon tree in the front sparkled with white lights, and on the dais next to the podium were the four Advent candles. People wearing coats and scarves were streaming down the aisles, and most of the seats were filled. As we came in, the minister took the microphone to be heard over the buzz of conversation.

"Everyone please snuggle a little bit closer to your neighbor, so we can make room for our many worshippers this afternoon," she said with a smile.

Colleen waved excitedly to me from her seat, pointing to the spaces she'd saved for us, and we threaded our way over. I slid into the pew next to Colleen and Daddy sat next to me. Lynn sat on the end and waved hello to Colleen's dad and stepmom down the row. Colleen had scoped out all the kids we knew from school and youth group, and she pointed out where they were sitting. There is this one boy Andy from youth group who everyone calls "Panda Eyes" because of his big, sleepy brown eyes and long eyelashes. He was sitting in the balcony. Colleen had had a crush on him for a few weeks. She'd been waiting for him to look down so she could wave at him.

During the service, we sang a lot of Christmas carols, and a member of the congregation lit all of the Advent candles. The minister gave a short sermon about Jesus being the sign of God's boundless love for us. While she was talking, I noticed Daddy take Lynn's hand. And then he took mine too.

We bowed our heads for prayer after the sermon, and while the minister said her prayer, I said my own. I said a prayer for Daddy and Lynn and for Diana. I said a prayer for Mama and Barry. I asked God to bless Grammy.

I should have said a prayer for Matt, but I didn't. I purposely didn't.

At the end of the service, we sang "Silent Night," and we lit our candles and held them up for the last stanza. Like our voices, the warm flickering points of light filled the church, all the way up to the balcony, and there was a hush of reverence after the last note sounded. I stood there basking in the warmth of love from all around.

When we got home, Diana was watching Animal Planet. Lynn started scurrying around the kitchen. She slid a turkey, beans, sweet-potato casserole, and some other side dishes she'd made earlier into the oven to warm.

"Stephanie, I want us to have Christmas Eve dinner together before you go to your mom's," she said. "Diana, why don't you set the table while Stephanie packs up her stuff?"

"We'll open presents after dinner, and then I'll take you over there," Daddy said to me.

I slowly went upstairs to pack my things. I put my weekend bag on the bed and stood staring at it. I was only going to be there for two days, so I didn't need to take much.

I dreaded seeing Matt.

One time, I had been dropped off early from cheerleading practice, and he and his friends had been drinking beer in the basement. Standing at the top of the stairs, I'd overheard them talking and laughing.

" ... and I had just gotten a case out of the fridge when Matt accidentally hit the garage door opener—"

"— and you thought the people were home—"

"— and I dropped the case right on my foot!"

"What an idiot!"

After listening for a few minutes, I figured out that they had stolen the beer from someone's garage refrigerator. I was getting ready to go back to my room when Matt suddenly cracked the door open and poked his head through. He had a square face, like my stepdad's, but he was shorter and heavier than Barry. His breath smelled horrible. "What did you hear, you little twerp?"

"Nothing." My throat went dry, and I put my hands behind my back to keep him from seeing that they'd started shaking.

"I don't believe you." He put his face close to mine. "If you tell, you'll be sorry," he said in a nasty whisper. "Do you understand?"

I swallowed but didn't answer.

He reached out and grabbed my chin. "Do you understand?" he hissed.

I'd wrenched my head away. And I did tell Daddy. But I'd made him promise not to say anything to Mama or anyone else. And I'd wished something bad would happen to Matt. I wished he would get caught and thrown in jail.

When I got back downstairs after packing, Daddy had put on a Christmas music CD and Lynn had lit candles on the table. I knew everything would taste really good at dinner, and I normally love sweet-potato casserole, but tonight I was feeling nervous about leaving and barely tasted anything.

After dinner, we brought our gifts to the living room and sat around the Christmas tree. I was feeling more and more depressed, but I was also kind of excited about the presents I'd gotten for everyone and was eager for them to open them. I had gotten Diana some earrings that looked like horseshoes. I was so happy that I'd found her something horse related.

"Oh, thanks," she said as she pulled the top off the box. She put them on and swung her head to show me.

When it was time for Diana to give me her gift, she handed me a bag with lots of green tissue paper neatly framing the top. Lynn was smiling with an expectant look on her face, and I suspected Lynn had helped Diana pick out the gift for me. I didn't know how I felt about that. I had picked out Diana's myself and had spent my own allowance on it.

But when I opened it I knew. It was a brand of perfume I'd sprayed myself with once when I was shopping with Lynn, so I knew Lynn had picked it out. Maybe Diana hadn't even had anything to do with it.

"Thanks, Diana," I said, and gave her a hug.

"Sure," she said, and after a moment of hesitation, she hugged me back.

Daddy and Lynn gave me a pair of black leather boots I had asked for.

"I love them!" I said, pulling them on. They fit perfectly. I jumped up and gave Daddy and Lynn hugs. I sat back down, admiring them, inhaling the rich leather smell. Then my heart started beating harder because I knew now it was time to go.

"Diana, why don't you open the present from your dad," I said, stalling, pointing to the shoebox-sized package that had come in the mail.

"No, I want to wait until Christmas Day to open it," Diana said.

"Oh, come on. I want to see what it is," I said. "I think I know."

"No, I'm waiting until tomorrow," she insisted.

I felt deflated. Didn't Diana know that I wasn't going to be here? Finally, I said, "Well, text me when you open it and tell me what it is."

"Well, I guess it's about that time then," Daddy said, glancing at his watch and standing up. "Is your bag ready, Stephanie?"

"Just a minute. I'll get it." I headed for the stairs. The heels of my new boots sounded much firmer on the wood floor than I felt.

In my room, I put the strap of my weekend bag over my shoulder, then looked around, reassuring myself that I would be back in just a few days. I picked up the shiny bag with my Christmas presents for Mama and Barry. Mama had told me that she would get something for me to give Matt, and I realized that wasn't any different from Lynn buying Diana's present for me. Except that I thought Diana and I had started to get close, and nobody would think that about Matt and me.

Downstairs, Daddy took my bag. "It's light," he said. "You'll have to come back soon, because you'll run out of clothes."

"Yeah," I said. I wished.

Diana was leaning against the counter and gave me a little wave. "Bye," she said. "Have fun."

Lynn gave me a big hug, patting my back several times.

"Have a wonderful Christmas, and we'll see you back here in just a couple of days." Lynn stood back and framed my face with her hands. "I know your mama will be so pleased to have you there."

"Yeah."

Impulsively, Lynn hugged me again. "Bye, sweetie."

"Come on. We better go," Daddy said.

For some reason I noticed how cold the car felt inside, though I hadn't noticed earlier going to church. I wrapped my scarf around my neck an extra time as we headed up the driveway.

"Need a little more heat?" Daddy said, adjusting the lever when I nodded. "So," he said. "What did you get your mama for Christmas?"

"She always likes to have parties out by the pool, so I got her a set of fancy painted plastic glasses. Do you think she'll like them?"

"She'll like anything from you, sweetie," Daddy said. "Well, listen, you'll have a good time. I'll be coming to pick you up day after tomorrow, and I'm sure everything will be fine."

"I hope so," I said.

"Are you worried about Matt?" he said.

"A little."

"If you have any problem, call me, you hear?"

"Okay." But I knew I wouldn't call, and I wouldn't say anything else about Matt. I was afraid I'd said too much already. I'd decided I'd just do my best to avoid him. We headed into Mama's neighborhood, with its tall stucco and stone houses, and I took a deep, shaky breath. When we turned into the driveway, I breathed a sigh of relief. Matt's black Mustang wasn't there!

Daddy didn't usually do this, but he got out of the car and reached into the backseat and got my weekend bag. "Come on, honey," he said. "I'll walk you in."

He put his arm over my shoulder as I headed into the house through the garage entrance to Mama's country-French-style kitchen. Mama was at the counter, dressed in a tight-fitting red top and black jeans, getting out bowls for ice cream. Her dark hair was pulled up into a pretty twist.

"There you are!" she said excitedly. "I thought you'd be here earlier. I feel like I've been waiting forever for you to get here." She ran over and gave me a tight hug, and I could smell her Chanel perfume. Then she stood back and held out her arms to Daddy. "It's Christmas Eve. We'll have hugs all around! Norm, you look good. Merry Christmas. Thanks for bringing her."

"Sure. Merry Christmas to you," Daddy said, hugging Mama carefully and then putting his hands in his pockets. When he was around Mama, he was quieter than usual.

She rushed back to the counter. "Stephanie, I've got your favorite swirl ice cream. Here are our bowls. And we need spoons!" The spoons clattered as she took them out of the drawer. "Barry is upstairs on the computer, and Matt is out with his friends, so it'll be just the two of us!"

"Matt is out with his friends on Christmas Eve?" Daddy said.

Mama waved a hand in his direction carelessly. "Don't ask me! His father told him he could, just for a little while. Apparently he still had presents to get."

"He didn't get presents yet?" I said, amazed.

"That's what he told his father." Mama rolled her eyes.

Mama's calico cat, Starbucks, came weaving into the kitchen and meowed at me. That was the one thing I wished, that I could have taken Starbucks to live with me at Daddy's, but Mama is attached to her.

"Hey, Star!" I scooped her up and held her in my arms, scratching behind her ears and under her chin where she likes it. Diana had been over here once for a few minutes, and she'd spent the entire time with Starbucks.

"And I got us *Elf*. You said you liked that movie with Will Ferrell, right, Stephanie?"

"Yeah." It had been on TV about ten times the past week, and I'd already watched it, but I didn't tell Mama that. I could watch it again. Starbucks meowed and jumped out of my arms, onto the floor, and then darted out of the room.

"Okay, I'm going to head out," Daddy said, putting down my weekend bag. "I'll be here to pick you up the day after tomorrow."

"Make it late, Norm. After dinner; I want her as long as I can have her!" Mama said, waving her arms at Daddy.

"Well, we were hoping Stephanie could have dinner with us, I think." Daddy looked pleasant, but he was impatiently turning the doorknob back and forth.

"No, no, no. I've got plans to take her out, and y'all had her for dinner tonight," Mama said, her hand on her hip. Daddy opened his mouth to argue, then shot me a look.

"Why don't you call me when you're ready, okay? Bye, honey." Daddy gave me a hug, met my eyes, and then closed the door carefully behind him as he left.

"Well!" Mama said, raising her arms over her head. "We have the evening to ourselves! I can't tell you how excited I've been, looking forward to this!"

"Me too," I said.

Mama rushed across the kitchen and hugged me again, rocking me back and forth. "And I've made plans for us to go shopping the day after Christmas, all your favorite places."

Mama and I always did have fun shopping together. I followed her into the den with my bowl of ice cream, sneaking a peek out the window for Matt's headlights. None yet.

She curled onto the corner of the chocolate-colored leather couch and patted the cushion beside her for me to sit down. "Let's not watch the movie right away. First I want to catch up. Tell me the scoop on everything!"

Mama always liked gossiping. I had grown up listening to her gossip with her friends, and I'd learned that I needed to watch what I said around her. Ever since I was about seven years old, I'd never told her anything that I knew had to stay a secret. Like how I felt about Matt, for instance. It was hard sometimes, keeping things from her, because I wanted to be able to trust her with everything.

She'd probably find out about Diana. She still talked to some of my friends' moms. She might already know about it.

"Maybe you already know … Diana got suspended. She got into a fight with another girl," I said.

"You're kidding!" Mama's eyes widened as she sucked the ice cream from her spoon. "How long is she suspended?"

"Five days is what they give you for fighting. The other girl got it too." I ate two bites in a row and then squeezed my eyes shut when I got a brain freeze.

"What were they fighting about?"

"The girl called Diana a name."

"What name?"

"Animal. It's something that kids in the school have started doing to Diana." Now I wished I hadn't started this conversation. I felt like I was betraying Diana, even though Mama would find out anyway. And I didn't even want to think about the thing that really made me feel guilty, which was the fact that "animal" had most likely come from something I'd said to Colleen last year after Diana was rude to me. I still hadn't admitted that to Diana. After all she'd been through because of it, I could only imagine how mad she'd get at me.

"Well, that's kind of odd," Mama said.

"Yeah. And let's see …" I decided to change the subject. "I got these boots from Daddy and Lynn for Christmas."

"Pretty." Mama glanced at them and nodded. They weren't by any special designer though, and Mama probably didn't like them. Sometimes she got jealous of things that Daddy and Lynn got for me or thought they were tacky.

"Oh, and the cheerleading squad is going to Disney World for a competition in a few months. Do you want to be a chaperone?"

"Oh, of course. Give me the dates, and I'll get off work! I can't wait!" Mama works a few days a week at a gift shop nearby.

Barry came downstairs.

"Hi, Stephanie. How's it going?" He's a pilot, tall with salt and pepper hair and a prominent jaw, and he's older than Mama. Sometimes I forget when he's home, because he spends a lot of time up in the upstairs TV room either watching golf or playing on the computer.

"Fine."

"What time did you tell Matt he had to be home?" Mama asked Barry.

"Midnight." He looked at his watch. "It's only nine. So he has awhile. I hope he doesn't come in late on Christmas Eve."

When I heard that, I decided I'd go to bed before midnight so I wouldn't have to see Matt.

"Okay," Mama said. "I'll have a breakfast casserole ready when everyone gets up." Mama held up her ice-cream bowl to Barry. "We're having ice cream. Want some?"

"No, thanks. I'm getting a beer," he said.

"Want to watch *Elf* with Stephanie and me?"

"No. On the Golf Channel they're rerunning a tape of the U.S. Open when Tiger won with a broken leg, and I'm watching that," he said.

He got his beer from the refrigerator and went back upstairs.

Mama and I talked about cheerleading for a while, and then we watched the movie. Starbucks jumped onto my lap and sat with me, purring. Halfway through the movie, Mama pulled me closer, and I put my head in her lap. She rubbed my head, making light, small circles on my scalp with her fingernails. I closed my eyes, just listening to the movie for a while and petting Starbucks, and then I let my mind wander.

At first, it always felt great to be with Mama. I felt like I was where I belonged. Then Barry would get involved, and then Matt, and everything would change.

Sometimes I was still awake when Matt got in, and he'd make a lot of noise coming down the hall, and I'd know he'd been drinking, though I never said anything to Mama or Barry. I figured they should be able to tell for themselves.

When the movie was over, I hugged Mama good night and went upstairs to my room and texted Colleen and some other friends. I turned out my light and lay in the dark, still texting for a little while.

I don't know how much later it was when the ringing of the phone woke me. I could hear Barry's groggy deep voice down the hall saying, "Hello?" Then I heard him say, "What?" in a loud and frightened voice. A few seconds later, I heard him and Mama talking in urgent voices, but I couldn't hear what they said.

Only a few seconds later, Mama raced into my room in her nightgown.

"Stephanie! We have to go to the hospital. Matt's been in an accident. Hurry and get dressed!"

She rushed out.

I threw back the covers and sat up so fast I felt dizzy. My heart thudded.

I grabbed the same jeans and sweater I'd had on earlier that night and hopped around pulling on my new boots.

Mama came to my doorway, yanking her arm into her red sweater. "About ready?"

"I don't know what kind of staff the hospital has on Christmas Eve," Barry said as he came to my door. "Let's go."

I followed them downstairs and slid into the back seat of Barry's SUV, still blinking sleep out of my eyes. Barry skidded out of the garage.

"Barry! Careful!" Mama said. "You'll have an accident too!"

Barry didn't say anything, just backed out, making the tires squeal when he switched into drive.

We raced down our street, past all the Christmas lights. One yard had a Santa and all his reindeer. The Rudolph had a blinking red nose. For some reason, it looked like a warning light rather than something festive.

"He lost control of the car when he was turning into the entrance of our neighborhood and drove into the stone wall," Barry said. "We'll probably see the car."

We turned out of the entrance and there, smashed into the stone marker, was the black Mustang, its hood accordioned and top flattened, the driver's door hanging open. The stone marker was demolished, with cracked and broken stones strewn on the manicured ground. A police car and a tow truck stood nearby, their lights flashing.

We all gasped. Barry slowed, then gunned the motor as he turned onto the access road. We sped through the quiet, dark streets and across the highway toward the hospital. Barry's driving scared me. He didn't talk. Daddy would have at least talked to us.

By the time we parked, it was starting to rain. Pinpricks of rain stippled the windshield and water glistened on the asphalt. We ran through the cold rain inside and were sent to the surgical waiting room, which had walls lined with cushioned orange chairs and two low round coffee tables piled with old thumbed-through magazines. A gray-haired man sat in one corner with his head in his hands.

After we had waited for a few minutes, a doctor in green scrubs came in.

"I'm Dr. Sullivan. Who's the next of kin for Matt Holson?"

"I am," Barry said, jumping to his feet. "I'm Matt's father."

The doctor shook Barry's hand, nodding. He was only talking to Barry, but Mama held my hand tightly as we listened. "Matt is still unconscious. He has serious head lacerations, as well as torn ligaments in his shoulder. His arm is broken in several places. It's too early to tell, but there may be neurological damage. He also has several broken ribs. One of the ribs penetrated his chest cavity and punctured his lung, causing bleeding and allowing free air into his chest. Breathing is very difficult for him right now. He's also lost a lot of blood."

"Is he going to live? Can we see him?" Barry asked, his car keys still in his hand.

"We are doing everything possible," said the doctor, "but it's too soon to tell how this will turn out. The first forty-eight to seventy-two hours are very important. We've taken Matt to surgery to evacuate the blood and air from his chest, but we don't know the extent of the damage and will have to determine that when he regains consciousness."

Mama squeezed my hand. Were we going to be allowed to see Matt? How would he look? Was he going to die?

I'd prayed for everyone in my family except Matt. I'd wished something bad would happen to him. Now something had.

3

DIANA

Christmas morning. Cold rain pattered against my windows. And I was suspended. I lay in my bed, thinking about other Christmases. One Christmas where Mom and Dad weren't speaking to each other. Five or six Christmases with just Mom and me in our little house. Each time, we'd opened our few presents for each other and then gone to a movie in the afternoon. It was depressing.

I wondered what Dad was doing today. Would he call me? I'd saved the gift he'd sent me to open today.

When I was young, I was so excited to open my presents. I could remember one year I just knew I was going to get a horse or a pony. And I *had* gotten a horse—only it was a plastic toy horse with a toy barn. I could remember my disappointment. It had felt like a stabbing in my heart.

Now I knew that I was probably never going to get a horse unless I bought one for myself when I grew up. But I had figured out that there were things in life a lot more important than the presents you got. Like someone caring about you.

And now this Christmas. At Norm's house. Well, Norm and Mom wanted me to think of it as "our" house. Or maybe Norm had changed his mind since I had gotten suspended.

Last year, Stephanie had been living with her mom but spent Christmas Eve and day with us. I hated to admit it, but having Stephanie here did make it more worthwhile to jump out of bed. But I remember feeling jealous of Stephanie, because having her here was what made it exciting for Norm and Mom. Whereas I was just the resident troublemaker with a mood disorder that they probably wished they could ditch somewhere.

I punched my pillow and turned it over. I heard Mom and Norm downstairs in the kitchen unloading the dishwasher. The phone rang, and Norm answered.

"Hi, Vicki, Merry Christmas. What's up? Is Stephanie okay?" The sound of dishes stopped. "Oh, that's awful!" Norm's voice rose in intensity. He said a few more things that I couldn't hear and then hung up, and I heard the buzz of voices as he and Mom urgently discussed something.

Curious, I got out of bed and went to the landing where I could look down and see Norm and Mom in the kitchen below. Norm was putting on his jacket. Their voices floated up clearly now.

"So she wants you to come to the hospital?" Mom asked.

"Yes. She and Barry are going to stay there. Vicki says Stephanie is exhausted, so she wants me to pick her up and swing by Barry and Vicki's to get her stuff, then bring her back here," Norm said.

"Oh, that's just terrible. I hope he's okay," Mom said. "And Diana's supposed to take drivers' ed next semester. I wish it wasn't so soon."

"That's the truth." Norm got his keys from the hook by the door. "Okay, I'll be back in about an hour, I guess."

He went out.

I headed downstairs. "What happened?"

Mom, who was getting coffee cups out of the dishwasher, looked up. I could tell from her face that something bad had happened. "Morning, sweetie. Stephanie's stepbrother, Matt, was in a bad accident last night. They've been at the hospital for most of the night, and they want Norm to come pick Stephanie up so she can get some sleep."

"Stephanie can't stand Matt."

Mom put the coffee cups in the cabinet. "Oh, Diana, don't say things like that."

"It's true! He treats her like dirt."

"It doesn't matter. It's still horrible that he's been hurt. I just hope it's not too serious."

"Once Stephanie told me she'd like to scratch his eyes out."

"Diana! Now you're just trying to shock me. Stop it. The poor boy is lying unconscious in a hospital bed. Show a little sympathy."

"I'm just saying."

Mom got a stack of bowls out of the dishwasher and put them away. "In all the excitement, I forgot to say … Merry Christmas!" She came around the counter and gave me a hug.

"Merry Christmas."

Mom squeezed me tight and gave me a kiss on the forehead. "Well, it will just be you and me for Christmas breakfast. I got a cinnamon coffee cake. Want some?"

"Okay."

When Norm brought Stephanie back from the hospital, she had big dark circles under her eyes and her hair was messier than usual. She curled up in the La-Z-Boy and pulled the orange-striped afghan that Grammy Verra had made over her. "I'm so tired. I feel like I have sandpaper in my eyes," she said.

"Are you hungry, honey?" Mom asked. "I have coffee cake."

"Yes, I'm starving. Staying up all night makes you hungry," Stephanie said.

Mom started cutting more coffee cake while Norm brought Stephanie's weekend bag back in.

"So what did you find out?" Mom asked Norm.

"He hasn't regained consciousness yet. He broke several bones in his left arm, and I guess he also broke some ribs and one of those punctured his lung. They had to remove his spleen last night. And he has a lot of stitches in his head. They are concerned about nerve damage to his arm, in addition to the fractures. It sounds like Matt is lucky to be alive."

"Did you see him?" I asked Stephanie.

She shook her head. "He was unconscious and was just getting out of surgery." She pulled the afghan more tightly over her shoulder. "It was scary."

"I'm sure it was," Mom said.

"They did a blood alcohol test on him," Norm said, pouring himself a cup of coffee. "He may have to go to court once he recovers. He could lose his license. We had to drive by the stone wall at the entrance to Vicki's development. It was almost completely demolished by Matt's car," he added.

"They towed the Mustang away, but you should've seen it. It was completely smashed," Stephanie said.

"Wow."

"You think about him being in it when it hit," Stephanie said.

"What we have to think about right now is Matt getting better," Mom said.

She set out forks and plates with coffee cake, and all of us sat at the counter while Norm and Stephanie ate.

"It's so scary," Stephanie said again, taking a bite. I thought about how weird it all was, because we were surrounded with the aroma of cinnamon and the lights from our tree were twinkling gaily, yet she was right— it was scary.

"You don't get along with Matt," I said.

Stephanie quickly looked at me with knitted eyebrows. Her expression said, *Don't say that!* I wondered if she was secretly glad that something bad had happened to him. But there was no way she'd say anything like that in front of the 'rents.

"Regardless of how we may have felt about some of the things Matt's done, he's in trouble now, and we want to hope for the best for him," Norm said.

For a few minutes we didn't talk; the only sounds were the dripping of the rain outside and the scraping of forks against plates. There was a charged atmosphere in the room, as if all of us were holding our breath, fearing that the world was a dangerous place and that random terrible things could happen to any of us any time.

"Why don't you go upstairs and take a nap?" Norm said to Stephanie.

"I will, but first I want to see what Diana's dad gave her for Christmas," Stephanie said, curling up on the couch again with the afghan. "I think I know what it is."

"What?" I said.

"I'm not telling. I'll just see if I'm right," she said.

"Should I open it now?"

"Go ahead," said Mom.

I picked up the package from under the tree. It was a little smaller than a shoebox and messily wrapped in brown paper for mailing, with my dad's rushed handwriting on it. I ripped off the brown paper and saw a cell phone box. Inside, nestled with a small softcover manual and a bunch of other papers, was a shiny black smartphone. I looked for a note from Dad, but there wasn't one.

"That's what I thought it was!" Stephanie crowed. "I knew it! He probably got you a plan too."

"Wow! Can you believe Dad did that?" I was so excited. He gave me a smartphone! Things really had changed. Now I could talk to him as much as I wanted. I checked and the phone worked.

"Very generous," said Norm.

"Yes, it is," Mom said.

"I'm going to call him!" I said. "He put his name first on the contact list."

"Oh, he did, did he?" Mom said, with a look at Norm.

I pressed his name and waited while it rang. After a few rings, it went to voicemail.

"I can't come to the phone right now," came Dad's voice. "Please leave a message." I was disappointed but took a deep breath and started talking.

"Hey, Dad, I just opened your present, and I'm really excited about my phone. Thank you so much! Merry Christmas! Call me back!"

We spent the rest of Christmas Day sitting around, eating, and talking on the phone. Norm made popcorn, and we watched *Miracle on 34th Street*. After taking a nap, Stephanie helped me program my cell phone.

Norm lit a fire in the fireplace, and we sat around it and let it warm our toes. Norm told stories about some of his favorite Christmas gifts when he was a little boy, like Rock 'Em Sock 'Em Robots and a model aircraft carrier. Stephanie talked to her mom several times about how Matt was doing. I heard her say he had had seventy-five stitches in his head.

We called Grammy Verra, who was at Aunt Carol's house in Virginia for Christmas.

"Merry Christmas, Diana. How are you?" she said cheerily when I got on. "Tell me what you've been doing to stay out of trouble."

"I know you say that as a joke, but I'm not staying out of trouble," I said. "I got suspended for getting into a fight."

"You what?" Her voice rose.

"A girl called me a name, and I threw a book at her, and then we got into a fight," I explained. "The vice principal suspended us both." There was a part of me that felt proud of what I'd done. I didn't care what Dr. Shrink said, I'd stood up for myself. I'd kept myself from disappearing. Of course, Norm didn't think that.

"Goodness gracious, Diana!" she said. "Trouble seems to follow you around. I don't know what to say."

"Nothing to say," I said. "It's pretty much a done deal."

"I must say this is the first time that any of my granddaughters have been suspended."

"I'm not really your granddaughter," I reminded her.

"Now, honey, let's not discuss that again. Of course you are. Well, do something productive during the days you're not in school," she suggested. "I'm heading back home to Emerald Isle tomorrow. Maybe you could come visit me. The beach in the wintertime is beautiful. So different from the beach during the summer."

After that, Stephanie talked to Grammy for a long time about what happened to Matt, and then she got on with Lauren, and they laughed and talked for a half an hour. Even though Lauren and I had finally started to get along okay on the cruise last fall, I didn't ask to speak to her. And I noticed she didn't ask to speak to me.

I wished I could go to the barn. I figured Josie was probably there right now, mucking the stalls and letting the horses out to pasture. If I were there, I'd help her and then maybe she'd let me ride Commanche.

By late Christmas afternoon, Dad still hadn't called. All those feelings I used to have about Dad not paying attention to me came flooding back, no matter how hard I tried to make them stop. I wanted to tell Dad about getting suspended. I thought maybe he'd sympathize. Mom had once told me that sometimes he'd gotten into trouble when he was young.

I went up to my room and called him again. I didn't want Mom to know. Still no answer. I hung up, deciding not to leave another message.

Still, he gave me a phone, right? That showed he cared about me.

I was lying on the bed staring at my phone when Stephanie came in and stretched out across the foot of my bed.

"This is the weirdest Christmas ever. It's like the normal parts of Christmas just kind of fade into the background because of what happened to Matt," she said. "Mama and Barry are just sitting at the hospital. I feel so guilty."

"Why do you feel guilty?"

"Well, you promise you won't tell anyone this, right?"

"Promise."

"I wished something bad would happen to him," she said, twisting a length of her dark hair around her finger. "And now something did."

So I'd been right. It made me feel kind of good to think that she wasn't perfect.

"You don't really think it was your fault," I said. "He'd been drinking, right? It was his own fault."

"In my head, I know that. But I still feel guilty. You're not supposed to wish for bad things to happen to people!"

"I seriously wish something bad would happen to that Carla girl who called me 'animal,'" I said.

Stephanie laid her head down and pulled her knees to her chin. "Well, that's different. Matt's my step-brother. I mean, I'm supposed to love him. But he doesn't love me."

I looked at Stephanie with her shiny, dark hair and wide brown eyes. "I've found that a lot of people don't like me, and they don't even know me. You can't make everyone love you, Steph."

Stephanie looked at me and pressed her lips together. "I hadn't really thought about that before, but I do want everyone to love me," she said. "I didn't know that was bad."

"Be like me. Don't care!"

"I can't help caring. Besides, you do care!" Stephanie said accusingly, sitting up. "You pretend you don't, but you do."

"Do not!"

"Do!" She pointed at my phone. "You care about whether your dad loves you."

I cradled the phone next to my chest. "Okay, I care about some people, yes."

We were silent for a moment. Stephanie knew me better than I thought. Better even than I knew myself, maybe. I had come to depend on getting her opinion on so many things.

At that moment, our doorbell rang.

"Wonder who that is, on Christmas Day," Stephanie said.

Norm answered, saying, "Well, hello!" Stephanie and I ran out to the upstairs landing to see who it was and looked down into our front hall. A group of dripping kids dressed in rain slickers stood at our door. Stephanie's friend Colleen, with her pink cheeks and straight blonde hair, was one of them.

"Hi, Mr. Verra. Stephanie texted me and said she'd changed her plans and was staying here over Christmas, right?" Colleen asked. "We're going caroling, and we were wondering if she could come with us."

"Hey!" Stephanie said, racing down the stairs. "How're you guys doing? You're caroling? Daddy, can I go?"

"It's raining!" Norm said.

"So? Even more need to bring good cheer," said one of the boys. I looked at him more closely and saw the uncombed blond hair and the silver earring. That new guy, Noah, from my Spanish class!

"Please?" Colleen begged. "She'll only be gone for a

couple of hours. My dad is driving us to the different neighborhoods."

I stood at the top of the stairs, looking down. It was definitely Noah.

"Hey, and Diana can come too." Stephanie glanced over her shoulder.

I saw all of them as they looked up at me. I saw the fleeting looks of avoidance and the quick effort to mask the way they really felt.

"Sure, yeah," said Colleen.

"Yeah," said Noah.

"No, I don't want to," I said. I walked back to my room and shut my door. Norm must have then asked the kids to come inside and sing a song for him, because I heard the faint strains of a very-enthusiastic "Rudolph the Red-Nosed Reindeer." One boy's voice was changing, and it cracked all over the place when he sang, "They never let poor Rudolph play in any reindeer games." I wondered if it was Noah. Then I heard Stephanie running down the hall. A minute later, she peeked through my doorway, holding her raincoat and gloves.

"You sure you don't want to come? We're only doing it for an hour or so. It'll be fun! A chance to get out of the house!"

"No," I said. I thought about Noah's face when Stephanie had said maybe I could come. Had he seemed like he wanted me to?

"Okay, but I'm not feeling sorry for you!" Stephanie said. "We invited you!"

She closed my door and was gone.

"You kids be careful," I heard Norm say, and then the front door shut.

I checked my new phone. Still no message from Dad.

Later, after Stephanie had come back soaking wet from caroling and had taken a hot shower, after Stephanie told me about the new guy named Noah, who had an opinion about everything, after Mom fixed Christmas dinner for the four of us, after we sat around and watched Christmas specials and I finally put on Dad's old Heineken T-shirt to go to bed, and after I was under the covers, groggy and half-asleep, Dad finally called me.

"Hey, dudette. How do you like the phone?" Dad sounded really happy, and his words were kind of running together.

I propped myself up on one elbow in bed. "I love it! Thank you so much."

"Great. I was pretty excited about it. I thought you'd like it. Yep, I thought you'd like it," he repeated. "Merry Christmas."

"Merry Christmas! I tried to call you earlier," I said, listening to his voice in the dark.

"Yeah, a couple of us went fishing today. You know,

a bunch of single guys on Christmas Day. A cold day out on the water."

I turned on my bedside lamp. "Did you catch anything?" Now that I was talking to him, I forgave him for not calling me before.

"We got a few pompano and flounder and then cooked them for dinner."

I didn't really know what kind of fish he was talking about, but pictured him twisting the hook out of a fish's mouth and tossing the fish into a bucket. I pictured him sitting around a scarred wooden table with other men, talking loudly the way he did sometimes, running his fingers over his reddish mustache.

"How's your mom doing?"

I didn't like it when Dad asked about Mom. She told me that he shouldn't ask about her, that he should only be interested in me. "Fine," I said shortly. Why didn't he ask me how my Christmas was, anyway? I wanted to say something that would make him pay attention to me. "Something happened to me," I said.

"What?"

"I got suspended for fighting in school." I waited for his reaction. When I'd imagined telling him before, I'd imagined that he'd be on my side. Now, suddenly, I was apprehensive.

"Fighting? What were you doing fighting?" he said impatiently, running his words together.

"A girl called me a name and I threw a book at her. Then we started fighting."

"Diana! What's the matter with you? Why can't you control yourself?"

"But she called me a name." I felt tears coming into my eyes.

"I don't care what she called you! You don't go around fighting with people. This is just another example of you flying off the handle. How many times do I have to tell you? Stop and think before you act. You're such a hothead."

Anger streaked through my body. "Mom says you're a hothead! She says I got it from you! I thought you'd understand."

"Your mother thinks I'm a hothead? This is rich. She's sitting there criticizing me to you when I'm not even there to defend myself. Well, I was going to invite you down during your spring break but under the circumstances, maybe that just won't work out."

He had been thinking about inviting me down to Florida for spring break? Why hadn't he said so before?

"What do you mean?" I could hear my voice rise. I was crying now. "I'll come down!"

The door of my bedroom cracked open, and Stephanie's concerned face appeared. "Are you okay?" she mouthed at me.

"I'm sure you don't want to spend time with a hot-head," he said, "so just forget it. And maybe you don't want to keep a cell phone from a hothead, so maybe I should just cancel your plan."

"Dad, no!"

He hung up. I threw the phone down on the bed and buried my burning, wet face in the comforter. I hated him, I hated him!

"Diana, what happened? What did he say?" Stephanie was next to my bed, and she put her hand on my shoulder. I was shaking. I just shook my head. I couldn't even put it into words.

I tried to think about last spring when Dad and I had gone parasailing, and we'd flown, attached to parachutes, high above the sound in the Outer Banks. Dad had taken my hand, and I'd felt so very happy.

"Diana?" I heard Stephanie's quiet voice and felt her soft hand rubbing my shoulder. "What did he say to make you cry?"

I sat up, wiped the tears from my cheeks. "I'm so mad. I feel like breaking this stupid phone he gave me. Why does this always happen with Dad?"

"I don't know," Stephanie said.

"I told him I got suspended, and he just started yelling at me. He didn't even bother to ask me how my Christmas was. He said he'd been thinking about inviting me down to Florida for spring break but now just to forget it."

"That wasn't very nice."

I lay down on the bed. Nobody could make me feel bad the way my dad could.

4

STEPHANIE

I sat with Diana for a long time, until she stopped crying. I don't know how late it was when I finally went back to my room.

I pulled the covers up to my chin and curled up on my side, thinking. Is it bad for me to hate Diana's dad? Once before, I had comforted Diana, when we were at the ranch and Daddy had told her she couldn't ride. I sometimes could feel Diana's emotions like they were my own.

What a strange Christmas it had been, with Diana suspended and Matt in the hospital. And Diana's fight with her dad. I felt like I should be especially good to balance out everything else.

When I woke up, I had a stomachache. Daddy and Lynn had to go back to work today, so Diana and I were here alone. I decided I'd get up and make waffles for us, even though I didn't really feel like eating them, and headed downstairs in my pj's and got out the waffle maker.

While I was mixing the batter, Mama called.

"Hey, sugar," she said. "How are you doing? I am so sorry we can't go shopping today the way I promised you."

"That's okay." I plugged in the waffle maker, then stirred the batter while squeezing the phone between my ear and my shoulder.

"They're still waiting for Matt to wake up," she said.

"That's awful," I said. I told myself that nobody deserved to have such a terrible thing happen. What if he never woke up? I shuddered. I poured the batter onto the hot griddle and shut the waffle maker, watching as a puff of steam and a glob of the yellow batter popped out around the edge.

"Barry is just a mess," Mama was saying, "pure and simple. I have to be the best wife to him that I can. I hope you understand that, sugar."

"Oh, I know," I said. "We can go another time."

Diana's footfalls sounded on the stairs, and she wandered into the kitchen. She sat on a stool at the counter, sticking her finger into the bowl of waffle mix and licking it.

"Well, maybe when things calm down a little you can come back and stay with us," Mama was saying.

"Sure," I said. Right now going back would mean sitting around the hospital in those orange chairs with the plastic cushions and watching people in scrubs hurry by. Every time they pushed someone down the hall on a gurney, I wondered if it was Matt and my heart would speed up. He wasn't my real brother. He was mean to me. I didn't even want to see him.

And then, the minute I had those thoughts, I felt guilty.

Mama said she'd call back when she could, and we hung up.

"Yum," said Diana. "You're making some for me too, right?"

"Of course!"

The little light on the waffle maker turned red, which meant the waffle was done. I lifted the waffle onto a plate.

"Me first!" Diana said, holding out her hand.

"Little piglet!" I said, handing it to her, and she gave me a satisfied smile as she opened the syrup. As I was pouring batter for my waffle onto the griddle, my cell phone chirped, telling me I had a text.

Diana picked up my phone and read, "'Hey, want me to bring my guitar over and play you a song?'" She looked at me. "Who's that from?"

"Let me see." I closed the griddle and took the phone. "Oh, it's that new guy who went caroling that I was telling you about. Noah. He got a new guitar for Christmas." He had been friendly toward me the whole time we were caroling. I had been nice to him but wasn't sure what to think of him yet.

"He's texting you?" Diana asked. Her face took on a hard look.

"I guess."

"Oh. Well, that's nice."

She was acting weird.

For some reason I felt like I needed to defend him. "You know his mom just married Kevin's dad and he just moved here, right? That's why he was caroling with them yesterday. He hardly knows anybody."

"Uh-huh." Diana focused on eating her waffle.

I opened the waffle maker and lifted out the browned waffle. "He said he's in your Spanish class."

"Yeah. When did you talk about me?"

"Just when we left, after he saw you from the front door. He seems kind of out there, like I said last night. He does not hold back."

"Norm and Mom won't let him come over when they're not here."

"Oh, I know," I said. I didn't even know if I wanted him to. Diana was definitely acting weird. "Is something wrong?"

Diana shook her head. "Nope. Just don't really like him."

"Okay." I put butter and syrup on my waffle and sat down to eat it. I still had a little stomachache. There was no telling what was going on with Diana.

Later, Josie picked up Diana to go to the barn, and I was home alone when my cell phone rang.

"Stephanie, honey?" It was Daddy. His voice sounded strained. "I'm going to need you to get your things packed to go to Emerald Isle to Grammy Verra's house for a few days. I'm on my way home right now and Lynn will be there soon. She's going by the barn to pick up Diana."

"Why? What's happened?" My heart pounded hard.

"Grammy Verra got sick after she came home from

Aunt Carol's this afternoon. She's been taken to the hospital. We don't know what's wrong yet."

"Oh no! Is she going to be okay?"

"We hope so, honey. I'll be home in a few minutes. Go ahead and get your stuff packed."

I hung up. Goose bumps traveled all over my body and my heart sped up. Grammy Verra in the hospital! Oh no!

I raced up to my room and started stuffing my things back into my overnight bag, thoughts whirling through my head.

Had an ambulance taken Grammy Verra to the hospital? Had they had to lift her onto a stretcher like they did on TV? Was there any blood? Was she in a lot of pain? Would she have to have surgery?

I changed my mind. I dragged my big blue suitcase out of my closet.

In my whole life, I had never seen Grammy Verra sick or in bed. I always thought of her as strong and in charge. Thinking of her in a hospital bed made me feel scared. Like some part of the world wasn't right any more.

I sat down on my bed.

The summer that Mama and Daddy decided to separate, I had gone to Grammy Verra's house to stay for a while. She lived in a sunny two-bedroom condo not far from the beach at Emerald Isle. Even though I'd had my own bedroom, most of the nights I would sleep in Grammy's bed with her. I'd fall asleep with her rubbing my back and talking softly to me. During the day, she took me out on the beach where she sat under an umbrella while I built sandcastles. She also signed me up for a sea-turtle program at the aquarium at Pine Knoll Shores and went with me when we strolled the beach looking for sea-turtle nests. Most of all, she talked with me about Mama and Daddy.

"What did I do wrong?" I'd asked her. "Is this because of me?"

"Absolutely not. It has nothing to do with you, honey," she said. "They may not be able to live together anymore, but they both still love you more than words can say. And that will never change."

And during those two weeks I stayed with Grammy, I felt like Grammy would be there for me no matter what happened with my parents. Her condo became a safe place for me. When Mama had come to pick me up, I clung to Grammy, not wanting to go with Mama. I remembered those two weeks with Grammy just like they were yesterday, even though it had all happened when I was in fifth grade.

I started packing my sweatshirts and socks. It seemed like all I'd done for the past few days was pack and unpack. First packing to go to Mama's. Then packing to come back here. Now packing again to go to Grammy Verra's.

Would Grammy need surgery? Grammy Verra was old. Wasn't anesthesia more dangerous for old people?

My phone rang. It was Noah.

"You didn't answer my text message so I decided to call you instead," he said. "Hope that's okay. I'm learning 'Hey Jude' by the Beatles, and I was wondering if I could come play it for you."

Oh no. Could he have a crush on me? Had I led him on? I'd have to be careful about how I talked to him.

"I'm sorry I didn't answer," I said. "There's a lot going on." I made a neatly folded pile of my tops and put them in the suitcase on top of my sweatshirts.

"Is everything okay? You sound funny," he said.

"It's just … my grandmother just got taken to the hospital. We have to leave today to go to her house."

"Oh, man. Sorry."

"Yeah, me too. I'm really worried about her."

"Where does she live?"

"Emerald Isle."

"How far away is that?"

"About five hours."

"Oh. So do you think you'll be there for the rest of Christmas vacation?"

"I have no idea. This is all really sudden."

"Okay, well." His voice kind of dropped with disappointment. "I hope everything is okay with your grandmother."

"Thanks. Talk to you later."

I tossed my phone on my bed. He definitely had a crush on me. He'd been hoping to get together sometime before break was over. Had I led him on? I could feel my cheeks get warm when I thought about it. Maybe I should stop being nice to him. It was good that I was going to be gone for a few days.

By the time the garage door opened and Daddy came in, my big blue suitcase was packed, and I was downstairs waiting for everyone. He said "Hi," really quickly, pulling off his tie, and hurried back to his room to pack his own things. I had all kinds of questions to ask him, but I knew not to ask them right now.

A few minutes later, Lynn and Diana came in.

"Why do I have to go?" Diana stopped in the doorway and pulled off one riding boot. "She's not my real grandmother. I only met her twice."

"The whole family is going, Diana. She's Norm's mother, and we love her and want to be there for her."

"I'm going to call Dad." Diana hopped around, pulling off a second riding boot. "Maybe he'll let me fly down to Florida to stay with him."

"No, we're not doing that," Lynn said matter-of-factly. "Go upstairs and pack enough for at least three or four days. Hurry up."

"Why not?" Diana dropped her boot on the ground.

"It's a bad idea for so many reasons I can't even list them all," Lynn said. "I don't have time to discuss this. I've got to go pack my things." Lynn left her purse and keys on the kitchen table and, taking off her white coat, went back into the master bedroom.

Diana stomped past me and up the stairs.

"I don't care what she says, I'm calling Dad."

"It's too late to get a plane ticket," I said, following her upstairs. "We don't even have time to take you to the airport. And what if your dad doesn't want you to come?"

"He just gave me that phone. He would want me to come."

I felt like Diana lived in a dream world when it came to her dad. Hadn't she just cried herself to sleep last night about him?

I followed her down the hall to her bedroom. The walls were covered with horse posters. An old bridle that was turning greenish hung over the mirror above her dresser.

"I'm already packed. I can help you," I said.

Diana didn't respond. She had her phone to her ear.

"Dad, I'm sorry I said you were a hothead." She took a breath and started pacing the room. "I need to come down to visit you because the rest of the family has to go to Emerald Isle because Norm's mom is in the hospital. You said you wanted me to come before. Can you call me back?" She tossed the phone on her bed. "They can't make me go!"

Hot anger flashed through my body. I pulled Diana's suitcase out of her closet and threw it onto her bed. I loved Grammy Verra! I couldn't believe Diana was acting like this. "Grammy Verra's in the hospital! Can't you think about anybody besides yourself?"

Diana whirled around, her hands on her hips. "You have no idea how I feel. I've met her for a total of a week out of my entire life and now I have to go spend my Christmas break sitting around a hospital!"

I did know how she felt. That was exactly what I had been thinking about Matt. But I didn't say anything about that to her.

"You got along with Grammy great!" I said instead. "You talked about how much you both love animals. And she hugged you and you let her, I saw you!"

I thought about Grammy being in the hospital and wondered if she was in pain. I didn't want to see her lying in a hospital bed. Would she have tubes everywhere? What if she died?

Diana marched to the window and stared out. "So what? She's not my grandmother."

I thought of something that might convince her. "While she's in the hospital, we'll probably have to watch her dog, Jelly."

Diana turned to gaze at me, excitement beginning to spread across her face. "We'll get to live with a dog?"

She threw two pairs of wadded-up jeans into her suitcase, then tossed in three sweatshirts.

5

DIANA

All four of us were in Norm's car, on our way to Emerald Isle. Norm and Mom, up front, talked urgently about hospital visiting hours and other logistical things. Stephanie's phone kept beeping with texts from that new kid, Noah, and she was ignoring them and trying to hide it from me. Like I cared!

"I don't care if you text with that guy," I said. "I just don't really like him, that's all."

"Why don't you like him?"

"He asked me about being called 'animal,' and said I should punch Carla."

Stephanie cocked her head thoughtfully. "You can't blame him for what you did yourself."

"Whatever." I looked out the window. I was never going to tell her that at first I kind of thought he liked me, but now it was obvious he liked her.

"Come on, buddy! While we're young!" Norm snapped at the driver in front of us. He was driving faster than usual and had twice blown the horn at someone.

"Calm down, Norm," Mom said. "We'll get there when we get there."

I was checking my phone every few minutes, but Dad hadn't called me back. Was he still mad? My eyes still throbbed from crying so much last night. It was his fault. He'd called me a hothead first.

Maybe there was an airport near Grammy's house, and Mom and Norm could take me to catch a flight to Florida once we got there. But I could tell Norm was in a bad mood. I'd have to talk to Mom about it. Later.

"So what kind of dog is Jelly?" I asked Stephanie, poking her with the toe of my sock. We'd both taken off our shoes in the car.

"He's part Chihuahua and part dachshund," she said. "Grammy calls him a Chiweenie. He looks like a Chihuahua with a long body and short legs. And Grammy talks about how sweet he is, but he is the grumpiest dog ever. He growls when you try to pet him. And he stinks even though Grammy is always giving him baths."

"Doesn't he sound fabulous?" Norm interjected with a laugh, looking at us in the rearview mirror. "How could a person live without such a dog?"

"Ah, yes, the lovable Jelly," Mom said, laughing.

"I'll get him to like me," I said. "That's one of my talents, getting animals to like me. Do you have a picture of him?" I asked Stephanie.

"No, but Grammy has about a million around her apartment."

"Maybe he'll sleep on my bed," I said. "I'm calling dibs!"

"He'll never sleep on your bed!" Stephanie said. "He's too grumpy!"

"How much do you want to bet?" I asked.

We were able to drive most of the way to Grammy's house on the interstate, but then we exited onto a two-lane highway with fields and farms on either side. The land flattened out. We passed white farmhouses that were in the middle of the fields and shaded by one or two giant trees. As the sun began to set, the winter sky turned pink with wispy indigo clouds, and the shadows grew longer. Norm slowed the car as we drove through a small town, past rows of clapboard houses, a school, a gas station, a church, and a small brick library. Darkness fell, and front porch lights and street lights winked on. We drove through the town and back out into the country, with only darkness outside the car window. Our headlights revealed empty fields ahead.

Norm and Mom, still talking about Grammy and the hospital, were ignoring us. Stephanie and I wedged our pillows into opposite window corners and put our feet up on the seat.

"I get the inside!" I said, pushing Stephanie's feet to the outside.

"Hey, I want the inside!" Laughing, Stephanie squeezed her feet in and pushed mine out.

"Inside!" I moved my feet inside hers and pushed hers out. I started laughing too.

"Girls! Quiet down!" Norm said, sounding irritated.

Mom glanced at Norm, then turned to us and held her finger to her lips. "They're just fooling around, Norm."

"They don't need to be horsing around in the car."

Dad's ringtone sounded from my phone. He was calling me back! I didn't want everyone in the family to hear what I said to Dad, so I turned toward the cold, dark glass of the window and talked in a quiet voice.

"Hey, Dad?"

"Yeah, what's going on?"

"Well, we're in the car right now, and the family has to go visit Norm's mom in the hospital, and since she's not my real grandmother, I was thinking that I could come down and visit you."

Stephanie poked me with her foot. I ignored her.

"What is she saying back there?" Norm said to Mom. "Who is she talking to?"

"Diana, are you talking to your father?" Mom said, turning in her seat.

Meanwhile, in my ear, Dad was saying, "You can't just make plans to fly down here on short notice like that, Diana. It's the holidays and all the flights are full."

"You could check."

"No, I'm not going to check. I already know this."

"Dad!" I could feel the tears starting again. Meanwhile, up in the front seat, Mom was talking to me, telling me that going to Dad's was out of the question. I glanced over at Stephanie, who was chewing her nails, her eyes wide.

"Let me talk to your mother about this," Dad was saying.

I was not going to cry on the phone with him again. Biting my lip, I handed Mom my phone.

"Hello, Steven?" she said, her voice tense. Then she listened. "Oh no. Diana is coming with us. She could never get a flight at this point in time." She listened again. "Of course, of course. All right. Bye." She hung up and looked at me. "Diana, what in the world were you thinking, calling your father about going for a visit like that? I already told you that we weren't going to do that. You deliberately disobeyed me." She held up my new phone, then placed it in her purse. "Because you disobeyed me, I'm keeping this phone."

"No! That's my new phone! You can't take it away from me!" I sat up and tried to grab her purse.

"Stop it!" Norm yelled. "Sit back in your seat, Diana! We're not going to have a fight in a moving car!"

"You can't have my phone! It's mine!"

Norm suddenly put on the blinker and pulled to a stop on the side of the highway. He turned in his seat with a thunderous look on his face. "Sit in your seat, young lady. And your mother is going to keep your phone while we're at Grammy's house. We have enough tension worrying about Grammy's health, and Matt in the hospital, without you adding to it. Enough!"

Mom started talking to me, but I turned toward the dark window and put my hands over my ears.

I was not going to cry. They could not make me cry. I glanced at Stephanie, who was curled on her side of the car, trying to be as small as possible. As soon as we got to Emerald Isle, I was going to figure out a way to get away from all of them.

So maybe I couldn't visit Dad right now. I'd go somewhere else. People figured out ways to get away from situations and I could too.

I didn't want to go to the hospital and see all the sick people there. I didn't want to see Grammy lying in a hospital bed with tubes coming out of her.

I don't know how much later it was when we arrived at the hospital. I had curled up in my corner of the backseat for the rest of the way. Sometimes hot tears had leaked out of my eyes and rolled down my cheeks, and I'd had to wipe them away.

Stephanie was talking to Mom and Norm. I stayed curled in a ball, but I listened.

"Is Grammy going to be awake when we see her?"

"I don't know, honey."

"Is she in pain?"

"I think so, yes."

"I'm so upset," said Stephanie.

"Yes, me too," said Norm.

We were driving through another town and I glanced over at Stephanie. Streetlights shone inside the car and I saw tear tracks shining on her cheeks.

"Listen, honey, the doctors are doing everything

they can. We want to go see Grammy and let her know we're here for her."

"The girls are upset. Do you think it's a good idea to take them in to see her?" Mom asked Norm.

"I want to see her!" Stephanie cried.

I didn't say anything. Grammy Verra had been nice to me on the cruise. She had asked me questions about myself that a lot of other people may not have asked. She had given me hugs and insisted that I was her new granddaughter. She had given me advice but not in a way that felt pushy. Just caring advice.

But sick people scared me.

"I can wait in the car," I said.

"We're all going," Norm said firmly as he pulled into a space in the parking deck.

6

STEPHANIE

"Visiting hours will be over in fifteen minutes," a busy nurse behind a desk told us when we finally arrived at Grammy's floor. I wiped my eyes and tried to comb my hair with my fingers. I didn't want Grammy to think I'd been crying.

Daddy was walking ahead of the rest of us. I could tell he was very worried about Grammy. After what happened with Diana's phone, I was surprised that Lynn put her arm around Diana's shoulders as we headed down the long hall. I was even more surprised that Diana didn't shrug it off. I guess being in the hospital was scary enough that Lynn wanted to comfort Diana.

The halls were shiny green-and-white linoleum. Attendants in colorful patterned scrubs walked by on quiet shoes, carrying clipboards or pushing carts loaded with equipment. In the rooms, lights were low and tiny TVs hung from the ceiling. People in thin gowns with IVs lay in the beds. Trays with leftovers from dinner rested on rolling carts beside the beds, and the smell of the hospital food still hung in the air. I didn't like that smell.

In one room we passed, a group of people talked loudly and laughed, but the rest were quiet, with just the buzz of the television or the murmured conversations of one or two people.

This was the second time in two days that I had been in a hospital. It was so strange that Matt and Grammy were both in hospitals at the same time. Since Matt hadn't regained consciousness before I left, I hadn't been to his room to see him. I had only been in the waiting room. I was glad. I didn't know how he would look all bandaged up. Had he woken up yet?

"This is Grammy's room," Daddy said quietly, stopping beside an open door.

My mouth went dry. What would she look like?

Nobody talked. I peeked in.

Grammy lay in the bed, looking small and pale. I almost didn't recognize her. Her mouth, usually smiling and laughing, was a thin line without her usual lipstick. Her closed eyes looked large and sunken. An IV went into the crook of her arm, and she was hooked up to a monitor that beeped softly and continuously. She wore a faded hospital gown and was covered with a thin, stiff, white blanket.

Everything went blurry as tears stung my eyes. My breathing felt shaky. I blinked hard, because it would be terrible if she saw me crying. To make myself stop, I gritted my teeth.

I tried to keep from thinking it but couldn't help it. Was Grammy going to die?

Hesitantly, Daddy stepped inside the room. The rest of us stayed out in the hall. Lynn swiped a tear from her cheek with a crumbly tissue and cleared her throat. Diana, with a stony look on her face, stared at the floor.

Daddy stood next to Grammy's bed and started to put his hand over hers but then let his hand drop. Looking at Daddy, just standing there with his arms hanging uselessly by his sides, made my throat ache.

Suddenly Grammy's eyes fluttered open.

"Norm," she said faintly.

"Hi, Mom," Daddy said softly. "I didn't want to wake you."

He took her hand, something I couldn't ever remember him doing.

"You're here," Grammy said. "Oh, Norm, I was so sick." She shook her head, remembering.

"You're going to be okay now, Mom. I know it," Daddy said.

I could feel a sob building up inside my throat.

"Grammy!" I ran across the room and leaned in to hug her.

"Stephanie, watch it! Don't get tangled in the IV!" Daddy said.

"Hi, sweetie," came Grammy's voice, weak and thready. "Sorry to say it, but I'm not doing so well."

I stood beside Grammy's bed, holding her hand, which felt cold and limp and bony. Lynn and Diana came in and stood at the foot of the bed.

Grammy licked her dry lips slowly and carefully. "I guess they have to wait for the inflammation around my pancreas to go down, and they're giving me antibiotics to help. And some anti-nausea medication. I was so sick. I've never felt so sick."

"Oh, Angela, we're so sorry," Lynn said. "I know you'll be better soon."

Grammy closed her eyes again. Daddy patted her hand. "Listen, we don't want to tire you out. We can't stay too long anyway because visiting hours are going to be over soon. We'll come back tomorrow, and maybe you'll be feeling better. We'll just head over to your place."

"Oh yes. And Jelly," she said. "I'm so worried about him! My neighbor has him. You need to take good care of Jelly and tell him I'm going to be back in just a few days, okay?" Grammy lifted her arm and waved vaguely at Diana. "Diana, are you going to take care of Jelly for me?"

I felt my heart speed up, and my cheeks grew warm. Why wasn't Grammy asking me to take care of Jelly? Why was she asking Diana to do it? Diana had never even met Jelly. *I* was her real granddaughter!

I stared at Diana. She had made such a big deal about not coming and seeing Grammy, even though it was obvious that Grammy really cared about her. She was staring at the floor, but now she nodded. "Okay."

At that moment, an energetic dark-skinned woman in scrubs with short hair and glasses came in, pushing a cart that held a thermometer and other equipment. "Hi, I'm Candace. I've been taking care of Mrs. Verra."

"Hi, Candace," said Daddy, stepping away so Candace could stand next to Grammy's bed. She looked at Grammy's monitor and wrote down some num-bers. Then she used an electronic thermometer to take Grammy's temperature.

With the thermometer in her mouth, Grammy closed her eyes for a second and squeezed my hand. I put my other hand on top of hers and leaned against the bed.

"So how's my mother doing?" Daddy asked Candace.

"Still a little feverish," said Candace, making a note. "She came in with a lot of pain. We're hoping that the pancreatitis will resolve itself quickly, and we can get her feeling better soon."

"On the phone, the doctor told me she may have to have surgery," Daddy said.

Candace measured Grammy's heart rate, holding her fingertips over Grammy's wrist and looking at her watch. "You can talk to the doctors all about that tomorrow."

"Mom, we should probably go," Daddy said.

"You need your rest," Lynn added.

Daddy patted Grammy's arm and gave her a kiss on the forehead. "We'll see you first thing in the morning, Mom."

I leaned across the bed and laid my head on Gram-my's chest for a few seconds. I could hear her heart beating slowly. I could tell she didn't like us seeing her weak like this. Grammy was strong.

"See you in the morning." She squeezed my hand.

"See you tomorrow," Lynn said.

I waved at her, as she lay there in the bed and we headed out of the room.

We were quiet in the hall and the elevator, each of us thinking our own thoughts. As the elevator moved down, I started feeling afraid that Grammy was going to die. The very thought made me feel panicked and made my heart start to skitter along faster. She was my rock. What would I do without her? *Dear God,* I thought to myself. *Please don't let Grammy die.*

I wanted God to answer me, and in the quiet of the elevator I listened, holding my breath. All I heard was the ding as we arrived at our floor. But why should God answer my prayers, anyway? I only remembered to pray when I wanted something. When things were going well, I forgot all about him. I'm sure he could see right through me. I caught my breath, and tears began running down my cheeks. I was glad it was dark and no one could see.

Once we were back in the car, on our way to Grammy's apartment, Daddy and Lynn started talking about when Grammy's surgery might be and how long we may stay here.

"I can't wait to meet Jelly," Diana said.

I stared out the window on my side of the car and

didn't answer. As the darkness passed by outside, I could feel myself getting mad at Diana. All she could think about was the dog. She didn't act worried about Grammy at all. Plus, how could she have called her dad about going for a visit while our whole family was so upset about Grammy? Why did Diana always make everything about herself? Why did she always make such a scene? I was so tired of it.

Diana and I rode in silence the whole way, until Daddy pulled into Grammy's driveway beside her golf cart.

"Grammy has a golf cart?" Diana suddenly said, looking over at it.

"Yeah, most people in the development have one for driving around the neighborhood and going down to the beach," Daddy said.

"That's cool!" Diana said. I could tell the visit to Grammy's had just become more interesting to her. She was supposed to take driver's training next semester, and she couldn't wait. She wanted to be able to drive herself to the barn.

Grammy's front porch light was on, illuminating a bush with dark shiny leaves and round pink flowers by her front door. Daddy let us in, and we set our bags on the floor in Grammy's small kitchen. A sunflower dish towel was folded neatly over the stove handle.

Grammy had a sunflower theme in her kitchen. She also collected Chihuahua figurines and pictures. The walls of her apartment were a cheerful yellow. On her screened back porch, she kept a shell collection. When I visited, we went shell-hunting almost every day. I loved looking through and running my fingers over the conch shells, sand dollars, Scotch bonnets, and skate egg cases, and listening to the musical clinking noise they made when I sifted them together. I'd brought a sketch pad on my last visit and had tried drawing them. While drawing shells, it was easy to see the amazing patterns of nature. Maybe there would be a chance for a walk on the beach tomorrow, so I could find a shell to bring Grammy. That might cheer her up.

Jelly's empty dog bed was nestled in the corner of the kitchen beside the light oak table. Grammy kept a basket of toys beside the bed. A yellow, stuffed puppy with a chewed nose lay on top.

"Look," I said. "Jelly loves to chew noses."

"I'll go next door and get him," Daddy said. "Get ready!" He went out the front door.

Lynn headed to Grammy's bedroom, and I rolled my suitcase back to the spare bedroom where Diana and I would be sleeping. In here were two twin beds with green, white, and yellow flowered bedspreads and a bookcase where Grammy kept games for her grandchildren. She had Chinese checkers, regular checkers, Connect Four, and Jenga. She'd gotten them all used at flea markets. Her Chinese checkers board had a drawing of a Chinese dragon on it that I had always loved to look at. Once I'd tried to paint a picture of it.

Diana stood in the doorway. I didn't ask her which bed she wanted. I just put my suitcase on the one closest to the door, the one I always slept in. I didn't feel like talking to her at all. I still couldn't figure out why Grammy had asked Diana to look after Jelly rather than me.

7

DIANA

I couldn't wait to meet Jelly. As far as I could see, Jelly and the golf cart were the only good things about this whole awful trip. I started to unpack, keeping one ear open for the front door and the jingling of dog tags.

"I can't believe Mom took my phone," I said to Stephanie as we put our things in the low chest of drawers against the wall.

Stephanie's dark hair swung forward as she leaned

over the drawer, arranging her shirts. She straightened and put her hair behind her ear, but she didn't answer me.

I couldn't stand thinking about the hospital. The smells and sounds in there drove me crazy. And all those sick people! Sick and weak. I thought about the way Grammy looked, and I shoved the image out of my mind. She'd been nice to me on the cruise, but I couldn't think about that. I just wanted to get away. If only Dad had let me come down to Florida. Somehow, tomorrow, when they went back to the hospital, I was going to have to get out of it. Maybe they'd let me stay home and take care of Jelly since Grammy asked me to.

"That's pretty weird that Grammy asked me to take care of Jelly," I said to Stephanie while I was waiting to shove my jeans into one of the drawers.

Still no answer. Just careful folding and arranging her pink girly things. Well, fine, don't talk. I don't care.

The front door shut. Jelly must be here! I dumped the rest of my jeans and sweatshirts on my bed and ran out into the living room.

And there, with Norm, was a fat, little brown dog. He had the sweetest eyes, shiny and brown, in a Chihuahua face that looked like a seal's. And a long, low Dachshund body. As I skidded to a stop and knelt to pet him, he let out a growl.

"Watch it, Diana!" Norm started.

Before I could draw back, Jelly nipped at my hand with his sharp little teeth.

"Whoa!" I backed away, but Jelly still sat there with one paw up, his ears laid back, and his lip curled. The canine tooth showing was curved and yellow.

Mom was right behind me. "Be careful, Diana. He doesn't like you."

Doesn't like me? Since when did a dog not like me? I sat down Indian style on the floor in front of him.

"Hey, what's the matter? I won't hurt you. I love dogs. See? I'm okay." I held my hand out a few inches in front of his snout for him to sniff. He made a noise between a growl and a whine and snapped again, this time grazing the tip of my finger.

I yanked my hand back, rubbing my finger, tears springing to my eyes.

What was this all about? I didn't get it. Animals always liked me. That was what I lived for, animals gathering around me and giving me their uncondi-tional love. What was going on?

"I tried to warn you about him," Norm said. "He likes things on his own terms."

"Goodness, Diana," said Mom. "Get away and give him a chance to adjust. Maybe you came on too strong."

And then I heard Stephanie's voice behind me. "I just got a text from Mama. Matt woke up."

"Oh, that's wonderful news!" Mom said. "What a relief! Did she say anything else about how he's doing?"

"Just that he's awake and in a lot of pain."

"Poor boy," Mom said.

"Yeah," Stephanie said. I glanced at her, wondering if she was glad Matt was in pain.

Stephanie came and stood beside me and Jelly. "So Jelly doesn't like you, huh? He only likes Grammy. He adores Grammy."

I crossed my arms over my chest. "He just has to get used to me, that's all."

With a dry chuckle, Norm hung the leash on its hook by the front door. "Good luck with that."

I stood up, keeping my eye on Jelly. He watched me warily and gave another low warning growl. Then he wandered back to Grammy's bedroom and stood in the doorway, looking at her bed, which had Norm and Mom's suitcases on it, before turning to look at me. He waddled to the guest room and looked at Stephanie's and my stuff on the beds and floor, then looked at me again.

He wandered out into the hall, looked again at both doorways, and lay down.

"He can't figure out where Grammy is," Stephanie said. She used a high voice to talk to him. "Poor Jelly. Grammy's in the hospital, Jelly. You have to be patient. We hope she'll be back soon, Jelly-belly."

Jelly put his chin on his paws with a sigh, angling his brown eyes up at us in puzzlement.

"I wonder what it would be like to be an animal," Mom said. "He doesn't know why Grammy is gone or if she will ever be back. All he knows is that he can't find her now."

"I bet he understands more than we think," I said. It made me feel depressed that Jelly didn't like me. But I wasn't going to give up on him. I would make him like me.

"Hey, can I take Jelly for a walk?" I asked Mom.

"I walked him on my way home from the neighbor's," Norm said. "He's fine for now. Maybe you can take him tomorrow."

"It's late. Let's get ready for bed, girls," Mom said.

Stephanie quickly put on her pj's, crawled into the bed, and turned toward the wall with the covers practically over her head.

"What's wrong with you?" I said as I got out the old Heineken T-shirt of Dad's that I always slept in.

Stephanie didn't answer me. She just lay in bed.

"Fine," I said. "Don't say anything. I didn't do

anything to you." Her silent treatment was really annoying me.

Suddenly Stephanie sat up in bed, the covers bunched in her fists and tears streaking her cheeks. "What do you think is wrong? Grammy is sick, okay? And I love her! You act like you don't even care!"

I could feel the heat surging to my face. "What do you mean? What am I supposed to do?"

"Act like a human being!" she shouted.

Her words hung in the air. I felt a painful lump rise in my throat and the corners of my eyes burned.

"Girls, girls!" Mom came to the doorway of our room. "The last couple of days have been really stressful." Mom sat on Stephanie's bed and rubbed her foot through the covers. "We're so worried about Grammy and about Matt. We could say things that we regret. Let's try to calm down."

"I didn't do anything! She's just mad at me because I'm not crying!" I said. Stephanie was the one who had yelled at me, and Mom was comforting her. Not to mention the fact that I'd been snapped at twice by that stupid dog. Sometimes I felt like the whole world was against me.

"Diana, Stephanie has had a really tough couple of days. Have some compassion for her," Mom said. "Are you all right, honey?" she asked Stephanie.

Stephanie lay back down and pulled the covers over her shoulder, using the sheet to wipe her face. "I'll be okay," she said.

Mom stroked her arm for a minute or two, and then kissed us both and went back into Grammy's bedroom. Her voice and Norm's hummed softly behind the closed door. I took my pill, turned out the light, and crawled into bed. On the other side of the room, Stephanie was silent. My mind raced from one thought to another. What did a human being do that I wasn't doing? I hadn't done anything wrong. I turned my pillow over and lay my cheek on the cool side.

Outside our room in the hall, Jelly was snoring.

8

STEPHANIE

The next day, the sea grasses outside the window to our bedroom bobbed in a brisk winter breeze, and the sand sparkled in the filtered sun. Grammy had told me she loved the beach in winter. She said the beaches were empty, and she liked being able to let Jelly run. The ocean and sky, she said, were moody and beautiful.

I thought about Grammy lying in the hospital, and suddenly the lovely mood and thoughts vanished, and

I felt my eyes begin to tear up again. I remembered the fight Diana and I had had the night before. I still couldn't see how she could be so unfeeling toward Grammy. I didn't want to be around her. Everything she said and did grated on my nerves.

"How far is the beach?" Diana asked Daddy as we sat around Grammy's counter eating cereal. "I want to take Jelly for a walk there. Then he'll like me."

"Only a couple of blocks," Daddy said. "I think Grammy normally drives her golf cart down there."

"Ooh. Can I drive the golf cart and take Jelly for a walk?"

I felt like saying, "Grammy is in the hospital and all you can think about is how you want to walk the dog," but I just concentrated on eating my cereal.

"Not this morning." Daddy stood up, placing his napkin beside his plate. Of course Diana didn't even notice how different Daddy was acting since Grammy had gotten sick. He looked pale and drawn. He hardly saw us when he looked at us. "I need to get back to the hospital. They say the doctors usually come by mid-morning, and I want to be there to talk to them."

"Norm," Lynn said, "why don't I stay here with the girls while you go to the hospital?"

"But I want to go to the hospital," I said. I wanted to be by Grammy's side and hold her hand.

Lynn looked at me and put her hand on top of mine. "Okay, honey."

So it was decided that Daddy and I would go to the hospital and Lynn and Diana would stay at the apartment with Jelly. As I got ready to go, Diana lay on her bed watching me. I went through my clothes, trying to decide what to wear, but couldn't concentrate. I had a headache from crying so much last night. Just the decision of what to wear seemed overwhelming. And Diana watching me was getting on my nerves.

"You're still mad at me, aren't you?" Diana asked.

Sighing, I started to brush my hair. My usual response would be something polite like, "No, I'm not mad," but I wanted Diana to know the truth. That's what sisters did. They told each other the truth. "Yes," I said. "I'm mostly upset about Grammy. I've never seen her sick before, and it scares me. And I don't know why I expect you to be upset since you don't know her very well, but it makes me mad that you're not upset. And I feel guilty, because I felt so relieved to get out of going to the hospital to visit Matt. But if something terrible happens to him, it's going to be awful." I put my hairbrush down on the dresser and gestured nervously. "I can't talk about it anymore now. Maybe later."

I put on my coat, wrapped my pink scarf around my neck, and left her lying there.

"We'll call and let you know what the doctor says," Daddy said as he kissed Lynn good-bye. "And then we'll come get you for visiting hours this afternoon."

In the car on the way to the hospital, Daddy hardly talked. We had to drive across two bridges on our way, and each time, I looked down to watch the choppy, shifting whitecaps, thinking about how cold it must be. I didn't see any boats.

"I'm proud of you for wanting to come and be with Grammy," Daddy said as we crossed the second bridge.

"How long will she have to stay in the hospital?" I said.

"I don't know," Daddy said. "I hope we'll get answers to a lot of our questions from the doctors today."

I remembered then the feeling of panic that I'd had in the elevator last night, thinking that Grammy might die. I wanted to ask Daddy if Grammy was going to die, but I was afraid to. As if he were reading my mind, he reached over and patted my leg.

"I know you're worried about Grammy and I am too. We have to assure ourselves that she is in good hands and is going to be all right."

I nodded.

When we came to Grammy's room, a new nurse was efficiently changing a bag of fluids in Grammy's IV.

"Looks like you've got visitors, hon," she said, adjusting the IV and patting Grammy's arm.

Lying against the pillow, Grammy looked small and pale. "Hi, sweetie," she said. Her voice sounded weak. I took her hand in one of mine and lay my other hand over it.

"How are you feeling today, Mom?" Daddy asked.

"Pretty out of it," Grammy said.

"We're feeding her intravenously until the inflammation around the pancreas goes down," the nurse said. "And we're giving her antibiotics. Her doctor should be in a little later this morning." She made a few notations on the sheet on her clipboard, and then, with a warm smile at me, hurried out of the room.

"How is Jelly doing?" Grammy asked. She closed her eyes as Daddy and I pulled two blue chairs up next to her. "I'm so worried about him. He's not used to me being gone overnight."

"He was definitely wondering where you were last night," Daddy said. "

"Oh, my poor baby."

"But guess what!" I said. "He tried to bite Diana!" Gosh, was I happy to announce that? Happy because Grammy had asked Diana to look after him?

Grammy's eyes went wide. "Oh no!"

"Twice! He didn't get her, though. They were only little nips."

Grammy put her hand over her mouth. "That bad little dog! Was she teasing him or anything?"

"No, I just think she scared him. I'm sure he'll get used to her," Daddy said.

I wanted to ask Grammy why she had asked Diana to look after Jelly instead of asking me, but I could tell she was still in a lot of pain, and I didn't want to upset her. Now wasn't a good time to ask.

"Norm, remember Patty, the dog we had when you were growing up?" Grammy asked. Her eyes were closed, but she had a faint smile.

"Boy, did I love that dog," Daddy said. "I remember writing a poem to Patty when I was about ten. Let's see if I can remember it. 'My dear dog, Patty. She is not a fatty ...'" Daddy and I started laughing, and Grammy smiled at Daddy's terrible rhyme.

"But she was. Remember how fat she was?" Daddy added.

"That was the year I had a crush on Allison Rockwell," Daddy said. "On the playground I used to flirt with her by running past her really fast."

How funny to hear about my dad having an elementary school crush! I started thinking about how amazing it was that we were sitting here in Grammy's hospital room while Grammy was so sick, but we were still laughing.

Then Daddy and Grammy started coming up with more memories of Daddy's childhood, like the time he sledded down the hill at the golf course and cut his chin and the time he flooded the basement when he was washing his first car.

They kept telling stories until Grammy complained that laughing made her stomach hurt. About that time, a kind-faced woman with short, stylish gray hair in a white coat came in. A stethoscope was hanging around her neck.

"Hello, I'm Dr. Claiborne," she said, shaking Daddy's hand.

"I'm Norm Verra, Mrs. Verra's son, and this is my daughter, Stephanie," Daddy said.

"Hi, Stephanie," she said. "What grade are you in?"

"Ninth," I said.

"Oh, your first year of high school."

"Right," I said.

"It's great that you're here keeping your grandmother company. Mrs. Verra, how is the pain today? Are the pain meds helping?"

"Yes, it's a little better." Grammy tried for a smile.

"Well, we'll keep up with that" She turned to Daddy. "Your mother has acute pancreatitis, or inflammation of the pancreas, which was brought on by the passing of a large gallstone. A gallstone is a deposit that forms in the gallbladder, and when it passes out of the gall-bladder, it can be very painful. This is a very serious condition. As soon as the inflammation has gone down, we'd like to do surgery to remove her gallbladder so this doesn't happen again. Meanwhile, she won't be able to eat anything; we'll have to feed her intravenously."

"How long before the surgery?"

"That will be determined by how long it takes the pancreas to settle down. If all goes well, I would say in three or four days," said Dr. Claiborne.

"And then how long will my recuperation be?" asked Grammy.

"Oh, we hope to be able to do laparoscopic surgery, where we only make a few small incisions, so you should be able to go home the same day or the next day," said Dr. Claiborne.

"The same day!" Daddy said, amazed.

"Yes, hopefully. Let's see how things go," said Dr. Claiborne. "Right now, let's keep working on getting that inflammation down. You're lucky we caught this when we did, Mrs. Verra. I'll be back to check on you later this afternoon. It was nice to meet you both," she said on her way out.

"It's hard to believe I may be able to go home the same day as the surgery, considering the way I feel now," said Grammy.

"Well, you should start feeling better soon," Daddy said. "How about a nap?"

Grammy nodded, her eyes fluttering. "Okay. That sounds good."

Daddy and I fluffed Grammy's pillow and straightened her covers, and then Daddy went out in the hall to call Lynn. I sat in the chair, watching Grammy sleep. Her breathing was slow and even, and her face looked trusting, like a little girl's. There was a faded blue stripe on her blanket. A transparent bag hung from a stand beside her and dripped slowly, one tiny drop at a time, through an IV into her arm.

It was sort of dark in her room, but shining from between the blinds, bright strips of sunshine played across the foot of her bed, so I knew it was sunny outside.

Listening to the rhythm of her breathing, I got out my phone and checked my text messages. Popping up among texts from Colleen and some of my other friends, I saw another text from Noah.

"How is your grandmother doing?" it said.

I'd decided that I wouldn't lead him on, but he was being really thoughtful, asking about Grammy. So I answered, telling him that she would have surgery in a few days.

And then I got a text from Mama. It said, "So far Matt has not regained movement in his left arm."

9

DIANA

After Stephanie and Norm left, Mom and I decided to take Jelly to the beach using the golf cart. Mom grabbed her cell phone and the shell bucket from the back porch, and we put on our coats, gloves, and scarves.

When I approached Jelly with the leash, he growled faintly but allowed me to attach it. Outside, he jumped into the passenger seat on the cart, looking at Mom and wagging his tail. He ignored me.

"Look! He's used to riding in the cart," Mom said. "He knows we're going to the beach."

"Why doesn't he like me?" I asked. "Grammy asked me to take care of him. How can I when he doesn't like me?"

Mom shrugged. "I have no idea. You just have to hope he gets used to you, I guess." Mom climbed in the driver's seat.

"Hey, can I drive?" I said impulsively.

Mom looked at me thoughtfully, drumming her fingers on the steering wheel. "Well, you will be taking driver's ed next semester," she said. "Okay." She showed me how to use the key to start it and how to move the knob next to my knee to go forward or backward. She also showed me the gas and the brake.

"Duh!" I said. Who doesn't know where the gas and the brake are?

"All right then," she said, walking around the cart to the passenger side. She poked me. "Slide over."

I climbed over Jelly into the driver's seat, my heart speeding up. I was going to drive! I jammed the knob into the reverse position and pressed on the gas pedal. The cart leaped backward, beeping loudly.

"Whoa! Too hard!" Mom said. I tried again, pressing my foot more softly, and the cart began to back up, still making beeping noises. Jelly leaned against Mom, his ears twitching as he felt us moving, and she cradled him with her left arm, rubbing his head.

"Okay, watch for traffic before you back out," Mom warned.

As if I didn't know that! Besides, there was hardly any traffic on Grammy's street since it was a dead end.

"I know, I know." I came to a stop in the street, then moved the knob over to go forward.

"Okay, head down the street, and let's find the area where you can park the cart." The front window of the cart protected us from the brunt of the winter wind, but the air still felt cold and damp. Light-gray one-story apartment buildings lined the street on either side, each with two apartments.

I steered the cart down the street, going too fast at first, then hitting the squealing brakes, then going fast again, then hitting the brakes again.

"Whiplash," Mom said, grabbing the dashboard with a laugh as I sped up.

"I have to get used to it," I said. "Don't laugh!" I tried turning the steering wheel to the right and then the left, veering into the left lane, to see how quickly the cart responded.

"Diana! Stay in your lane!" Mom said. "Golf carts have to obey the rules of the road, just like cars."

"I know, I know. I'm just messing around." Mom always worried!

"You don't mess around when you're driving a vehicle. Even a golf cart."

The street ended in a small parking area next to the beach. Jelly jumped down, barking, as I braked to a stop, and Mom gripped his leash. I asked Mom if I could walk him, and she gave the leash to me.

In front of us, between two dunes dotted with clumps of sea grass, a white sand pathway wound to the beach. With excited little barks, Jelly pulled on the leash toward the pathway.

Our shoes sank in the sugar-fine sand as we followed the path down to the beach. A fierce wind blew, tugging at my scarf. The tide was low, allowing a long walk across the dark stippled sand to the water. Meandering just above the waterline was a dark frilly line of seaweed. The ever-moving water was gunmetal-gray, choppy, and had a lacy froth on the waves. No one else was on the beach.

About thirty yards away, splashing in a small inlet of water that was about three feet deep, was a huge, dark shape about the size of a Sunfish sailboat.

Jelly began to bark and pull me toward the splashing creature.

"Mom, what do you think that is?"

"I don't know."

We hurried closer. Jelly barked continuously as we

approached, and the fur stood up on the back of his neck. Fear pricked the back of my own neck, and my heart started to beat faster.

When we were about ten feet away, Jelly suddenly stopped barking and didn't want to go any farther. He planted his feet and began to actively sniff, holding his nose high in the air.

Closer, I saw the creature was shaped like a large dolphin, but it was black rather than gray, and instead of the dolphin's bottle-shaped snout, it had a shiny, rounded, bulbous head with a small beak-like mouth. Its mouth was slightly open, and I saw a neat row of small, sharp teeth. The creature rolled back and forth, and the two fins of its tail flopped frantically in the shallow water. Its top fin had a nick in the top, as if something had taken a small bite out of it.

Jelly stood quietly, sniffing, his fur still on end.

"Oh, Diana," Mom said. "I think it's a whale. Look, there's the blowhole."

At that minute, the blowhole opened and the whale breathed, a rushing sound of air, out and then in, loudly and quickly.

"Oh!" Mom stepped back, surprised.

Mom must be right. A whale! Right here on the beach. But why was it here? Something must be wrong.

"Mom, the water's too shallow for it! It needs to be in deeper water! We need to push it back out to sea!"

"I don't know if the two of us can manage that, Diana. It must be twelve feet long."

"But we have to help it!"

"But the water's freezing." Mom looked up and down the nearly empty beach. "Look, are those surfers down the beach? They're wearing wet suits. Maybe we could ask them to help. Why don't you run down and ask them? I'll stay here with Jelly."

The cold air burned my lungs as I took off running down the beach toward two guys sitting on surfboards in the water. I ran along the water's edge, where the sand was hard and shiny and wet. I stopped in front of them, panting, waving my arms.

"Help! Can you help us?" I pointed down the beach toward Mom and the whale.

The two guys looked at Mom, then slid off their boards and into the water, and walked to shore, carrying their surfboards.

"That a whale?" Both of the guys were lean and muscular, wearing black, fitted wet suits. The one speaking was African-American, with a dripping ponytail of dreadlocks. The other had a sharp nose, a small mustache, and a wet shock of light brown hair.

"Yeah," I said. "It's stranded in shallow water. We need help pushing it back out to sea."

"Sure, no problem," said the one with dreads. Both

of them hefted their brightly painted surfboards and walked rapidly next to me toward Mom and Jelly.

"I can't believe I didn't notice it before," Mustache said to Dreads. "I wonder how long it's been there."

Jelly started barking at the surfers when we arrived, and Mom had to pull his leash tighter and talk over his barking. "Thanks for coming over. We think this whale needs to be pushed back out to sea."

"Sure," said Dreads, and he kneeled and took some time to pet Jelly.

Jelly seemed to accept the surfers once they took time to pet him. He sat with his fat, little haunches on the sand, watching the surfers and the whale with a wrinkled brow.

The surfers laid their boards on the beach and stood at the edge of the water. There was an indentation, or small inlet, almost like a bathtub, of slightly deeper water around the whale. The double fins of the whale's tail flopped crazily, and it made high-pitched squeaking sounds. Periodically, a rush of air whooshed from its blowhole.

"Ready?" said Dreads.

"Watch that tail!" Mustache said to Dreads.

"Be careful!" Mom yelled over the wind.

They took a few steps in, then leaned over. Each placed two palms on the whale's side and, bracing their legs in the surf, began to push. The whale's tail flopped again, and they jumped back, staggering a few feet through the frothy waves.

They needed help! Without another thought, I ran into the water.

"Diana!" Mom yelled.

I shut out her calls, wading deeper, until I was next to the whale, by its head. The freezing water splashed around my thighs. Cold water streamed over my arms. Half of my coat was soaking wet. The surf pounded and roared.

"Okay," said Dreads. "On three. One, two, three!"

We all leaned forward, pressing our palms against the whale's rubbery side, and pushed with all our might. I took two giant steps, my feet sinking in the sand, and as the whale made whistling sounds, its fins seemed to dislodge.

Then a freezing wave came in and pushed the whale back where we'd started. It whistled again.

"Aww!" groaned Mustache.

"Again," said Dreads. "One, two, three!"

Again we leaned with all our might against the whale, pushing it deeper into the water. As I pushed, I looked into the whale's large, wrinkled eye. It gave a plaintive call, almost like a birdcall or whistle.

"We're going to get you back out there, buddy," I said. "Don't you worry."

We worked out a rhythm where we'd wait for each wave to crest and pass, then, just afterward, we'd shove, using the withdrawal of the water to help pull the whale out to sea.

After we'd pushed four or five times, a guy and a girl walked up.

"Move down," the girl said, and both of them splashed into the water. Their jeans turned dark halfway up their legs as they got soaked.

I was panting and my hands and feet were so cold I could hardly feel them.

"Okay. Wait for the wave." Dreads let his arm drop as if starting a race. "Go!"

I gritted my teeth and groaned as I threw every ounce of my strength against the whale's side. As the water drew back from the wave, we pushed the whale deeper, scrambling to make progress with our legs.

"Go, go, go!" yelled Mustache.

Suddenly the whale flicked its tail, trying to swim, and the guy at the end got knocked against Mustache. "His tail just nailed me!" he yelled, scrambling to his feet.

"Please be careful!" I could hear Mom's thin voice cutting through the roar of the wind and the waves.

Then the whale sank under the waves, gave a powerful thrust of its tail, and began to swim out to sea. As

I watched, a wave hit me and knocked me down. Water gurgled and boiled around my face, and I flailed, trying to get up on my knees.

A hand grasped mine and pulled me, gasping, to my feet.

"You okay?" said Dreads.

I nodded. The whale disappeared for a moment, then we saw its nicked top fin break the water as it swam. We all stood, dripping, with our chests heaving, watching the whale make its way back out to deeper water.

"We did it!" said Mustache. "What an amazing experience!"

"Nice work, guys," said Dreads.

"Yes!" said the guy who'd come with the girl, pumping his fist in the air.

We all stood and watched the gray water for a few long minutes, but the whale had disappeared. I had ignored the cold while trying to push the whale, but now that I was standing still, my hands began to ache and my teeth started to chatter.

"Diana!" Mom was saying. "We need to get you inside and get you dry."

But it felt great to be standing out here with my new friends, basking in our success.

"Wouldn't it be cool if the whale breached right out there, like it was saying thank-you?" said Dreads. We stood in silence, breathlessly watching the shifting waves, hoping that it might. But it didn't.

"Well, I guess it's gone," said the girl. "I wonder what kind of whale that was."

"I have no idea," said Mustache.

"All's well that ends well," Mom said. "Thanks to all of you."

Dreads and Mustache picked up their surfboards. "See you later," Dreads said. "Hey, wonder if we'll run into him later while we're surfing."

"He's probably over a mile away by now," said Mustache.

Everyone said good-bye, and we went our separate ways. I was shaking too much to try to drive the golf cart, so I let Mom do it. "We're going to get you right in the shower," she said as Jelly hopped up beside me. He leaned over and licked my coat.

"Hey, now that I'm a hero, Jelly likes me," I said. The ride home was even colder with the wind whistling around the glass windshield. I was shaking violently. "Wasn't that cool, Mom?" I said, my teeth chattering. "Wasn't that the coolest thing ever? We saved a whale!"

10

STEPHANIE

That afternoon, in the car on the way back to Grammy's apartment, I told Daddy I'd received a text from Mama about Matt maybe not being able to move his arm.

"That's terrible! Which arm is it?"

"His left."

"Well, if he's right-handed, he'll still be able to write and do some sports. Maybe he'll still regain movement."

"Yeah." I wondered if Matt would still be in the hospital when I got back. What I would say when I saw him?

Daddy glanced over at me, his eyes very serious, and he patted my leg. "This has been a pretty stressful couple of days, hasn't it, honey?"

"Yeah." A memory of Matt flashed into my mind, the one where he put his face right up to mine and whispered, "If you tell, you'll be sorry. Do you understand?"

A little shiver ran down the back of my neck. Why did I let him scare me? Was there a part of me that was happy that he couldn't move his hand? That felt maybe he deserved it?

And I was not looking forward to seeing Diana again this afternoon. To tell the truth, my track record with stepsiblings wasn't too good right now.

"Daddy," I said.

"Yeah?"

I hesitated. I didn't know exactly what I wanted to say to him. Plus, he was already tense about Grammy, and I didn't want to worry him more. Finally I said, "What do you think about Diana and Lynn staying home from the hospital today?"

Daddy was driving across the first bridge over the water, and I looked over at the grayish-green waves at an ugly industrial area with a tall mountain of sand. "You have to remember that they don't know Grammy the way we do. You've grown up with Grammy. Diana and Lynn have only known her for a little while. Don't hold it against them, Stephanie."

"Okay," I said. But I realized I *was* holding it against them. I didn't think they were being loyal enough to Grammy. Especially Diana. Grammy had been so kind to her!

As if reading my mind, Daddy added, "It's not our place to judge others for what they do or don't do." He looked over at me and smiled. "Leave that to God. Plus, think of it this way. This morning you and I got private time with Grammy. And they'll go to the hospital tonight when we go back."

I nodded as we passed a surf shop that was closed for the winter. Shiny plastic mannequins wearing bikinis and surfer jams seemed to be shivering in the frosty window. A big sign said, REOPENING EASTER WEEKEND. I knew Daddy was right. I needed to stop being mad at Diana. Telling myself that and doing it weren't the same though.

When we arrived back at the apartment, the aroma of chicken soup surrounded us. Diana was sitting on the couch with wet hair, wrapped in a blanket, eating a bowl of soup, while Lynn stirred the pot by the stove.

In a closet in the corner of the kitchen, Grammy's dryer clanked and whirred. It sounded like a pair of shoes was in there, thudding as the dryer turned.

Jelly ran to the door when we came in, but when he saw it was us, his head drooped, and then he waddled back down the hallway and plunked himself down outside Grammy's bedroom with a loud sigh.

"How is Grammy? Want some chicken noodle soup?" Lynn asked.

"Sure," Daddy said. "She's resting right now. We met with the doctor, a Dr. Claiborne. They don't have visiting hours again until tonight. I tried to call you earlier." Daddy took off his coat and hung it on the coat tree next to the door. Then he headed to the kitchen and started helping Lynn get out spoons and napkins and bowls.

"You'll never believe what we did!" Diana said. "We saved a whale!"

"Really?" I said.

"Yes! There was a whale in the shallow surf, and we got some surfers to help us, and we pushed it back into deeper water, and it swam away."

"You went in the ocean in the winter? You touched a whale?" My heart tripped.

"Yeah! It was so amazing!"

"She ran in before I could stop her," Lynn said. "It was terrifying."

Now, as Lynn ladled soup for everyone and set it on the counter, Diana described how Jelly had barked, how she had run down the beach to get the surfers, and how another couple had stopped to help.

"What did it feel like to touch a whale?" I asked. "Did it have big teeth?"

"Like an inner tube," Diana said. "And yes, it had big teeth. Not as big as a shark's though. It flipped its tail and knocked one guy down. But it wasn't that big, maybe about twelve feet long."

"That's huge!"

"And it had a nick in its top fin, like another fish had taken a little bite out of it. I think I'm going to name it Nick."

"Nick the whale," Daddy said. "Sounds like a typical Diana adventure! You're very lucky that tail didn't get you."

"Mom," said Diana, "I want to take Stephanie out on the beach and show her where Nick was."

"Your hair is still wet," Lynn said. "Not to mention your coat and shoes and jeans." She pointed at the dryer, which was still making a rhythmic booming sound as Diana's running shoes tumbled around. "Let's all have some soup right now."

Diana had clearly forgotten that I was mad at her.

After we finished our soup, Diana and I loaded the

dishwasher while Daddy and Lynn talked in the living room about what the doctor had said about Grammy's surgery.

I just wanted to be alone. Back in our bedroom, I got out the colored pencils I'd brought, thinking that I'd try drawing one of the shells that Grammy kept in a basket on her back porch. Shivering out on the screened back porch, I sifted through the shells, listening to the soothing sound as they clinked together. I found a pinkish-white conch shell with a pattern of sharp spines along the edge of the opening. Grammy had bought it for me at a shell store when I fell in love with it. That had been that summer I'd stayed with her while Mama and Daddy were deciding to separate.

I brought that shell and a few others back into the bedroom and arranged them on the end table for a still life.

Diana came in, dropping her wet towel on the floor and flopping onto the bed. She grabbed her hairdryer and turned it on, the sound of the dryer blasting my concentration.

I tried to block it out, focusing on the curve of the shell and the way the pale winter sunlight shone on its bumpy surface. It was like Diana was following me around. I thought about what Daddy had said and drew a deep breath, trying not to be mad. The thing that made me maddest was that she didn't even seem to notice I was avoiding her.

It didn't take long for her to dry her flyaway hair.

I thought she'd leave then, but instead she lay on her side, propping her cheek on her palm. "Nick the whale reminded me about that preppie guy named Nick who you met at the ranch two summers ago," she said. "Do you ever text him?"

"Not for a long time," I said, still sketching. "Not since I saw him at that soccer game where we played his school."

"Then it made me think of Russell," she said. "I wonder how he's doing."

I put down my pencil with a sigh and pushed my hair behind my ear. "You could write him, using the address at the ranch. Or write Maggie." Maggie had been the head wrangler at the ranch. She'd had a special relationship with Diana, and she'd helped me lose a little of my fear of horses.

"I did write him. He never wrote back. Anyway, he's probably forgotten all about me."

I glanced over at her. "How could he forget you? With all the searching for the wolves and the surgery with Doc?"

"Or maybe he just remembers how mad he was at me."

"He's had time to forgive you. And now both the wolves are safe. You should write him again."

At that moment, the clothes dryer buzzed from the kitchen, and Diana jumped up and ran down the hall. A few minutes later, she was back in the bedroom, her arms full of her shoes and jeans, and she dressed to go outside.

"Come on, let's go down to the beach, and I can show you where the whale was. I can drive the golf cart."

I slowly put away my colored pencils. She was never going to get the hint.

Then Daddy was standing in the doorway of the bedroom. "Why don't you go down to the beach with her, Stephanie? A little fresh air will do you good."

I stood up. Nobody was leaving me alone.

"Now, I can't believe I'm having to say this, but don't go in the water again!" Lynn warned Diana as we put on our scarves and gloves. I shoved my cell phone in my pocket.

"And be careful with the golf cart," Daddy said.

"Okay, okay," Diana said.

Outside, the sea oats beside the house bent low in the wind. The sky was bright blue with thin sunlight streaming through wispy clouds.

"Hop in!" Diana said as she slid behind the wheel.

I climbed in the passenger seat, beginning to feel excited. The wind seemed to blow the cobwebs from my head. The past few days, I had spent a lot of time in the hospital. Maybe I did just need to go have some fun.

"Whee!" Diana backed out of the driveway at record speed, slammed on the brakes, and began speeding headlong down the sandy road toward the beach.

My scarf and hair blew out behind me, and I leaned out to the side, holding onto the windshield brace. "Wahoo!" I yelled.

The road ended in a small parking lot next to the beach, but Diana didn't stop. She just drove the cart over the mound of sand, past the sign that said No Vehicles, and down the path to the beach.

"Whoa!" The cart bounced so hard I almost fell out.

Diana drove down to an area near the breakers. "Here's where Nick was. The tide's come in since then. It took us about seven or eight tries to finally get him back in deep enough."

With a wrenching turn, Diana turned right and started speeding down the empty beach. Far away down the beach was the pier. It was so tiny we could barely see it. The wind whipped tears to my eyes and the end of my nose tingled with cold.

"Okay, I'm going to go as fast as I can go! All the

way to the pier!" Diana shouted over the wind, pushing her foot to the floor. The cart sped up, and we were flying over the sand. She zigzagged around clumps of seaweed. Three sandpipers frantically ran away from our tires.

I clung to the brace beside the windshield. I wanted to shut my eyes, but I was afraid to. The beach in winter was a different place. There was absolutely no one out here. The majestic gray-green ocean stretched out across the horizon as far as I could see, a bone-chilling damp wind whistled by, and closed-up houses nestled behind the dunes.

I thought of the many times I'd come out to this beach with Grammy, building sand castles while she read her history novels, walking out on the pier, and leaning over to look into the plastic buckets to see what fish people had caught. Once, when Daddy and I were staying here with Grammy, we saw someone catch a baby hammerhead shark. We'd watched in fascination and horror as it flopped around on the worn, warped wood of the pier.

"Yahoo!" Diana yelled again. She started turning the cart in big S curves, and I slid across the seat and crashed into her. I started laughing and realized it had been a couple of days since I'd laughed.

"Hey! Oh, my gosh. What's that?" Diana suddenly

said, pointing. I looked down the beach and saw something huge and black, like a giant tree trunk, lying on the beach a few yards from the water. We raced toward it.

As we approached, my breath caught in my throat. Shiny, black skin; a big anvil-shaped tail slowly flopping. I glanced at Diana. She braked to a noisy stop, jerking me forward, and leaped out.

Covering her mouth with one hand, she pointed with the other to the wilting triangular fin on top. A jagged nick.

"Oh no! It's Nick! He's stranded again!"

11

DIANA

I knelt by Nick's head and stared at the slightly open mouth with its neat row of teeth. And then, just above and outside the mouth, I saw his eye. Surrounded by wrinkles, it was dark blue and three times the size of a human eye. The wrinkles made the expression in the eye seem amazingly wise and sorrowful.

The same kind look I saw in Commanche's brown eyes.

And then the eye blinked. And Nick gave a plaintive, sad cry that sounded like a bird.

"What are you doing back up here, buddy?" I said, stroking the round knob of his forehead. "Why did you do this again?" I stood up, feeling breathless and panicked. "Stephanie! What can we do? He's stuck on the sand this time."

Stephanie came around to stand beside me. I could tell she was scared. She stayed a good distance away from Nick.

And then we heard a whoosh of air, a sound like a giant sigh, coming from a spot on the top of Nick's head. Stephanie jumped with surprise.

"It's breathing!" she said.

"Steph, we have to help him!"

"What can we do? I bet he weighs five hundred pounds or more! We can't move him."

I looked all around. The surfers had gone in. There wasn't another soul on the beach. "Maybe we can call someone. Did you bring your cell phone?"

"Yeah." Stephanie reached in her pocket and pulled it out. "Who should I call?"

"The police, I guess. Here, I'll talk." I took her phone and dialed 911. When the dispatcher answered, I said that we'd found a stranded whale on the beach. The dispatcher asked for my location, and Stephanie told me Grammy's address, since we weren't that far away. The dispatcher said she'd contact the Marine Mammal

Stranding Network and that someone would be here in thirty minutes to an hour.

"Meanwhile," she said, "do you have wet towels or a bucket? You need to keep the whale wet. Keep pouring water on the whale, and put wet towels on it to keep its skin from drying out."

"Thanks!" I hung up and got the shell bucket from the back of the golf cart. "Someone will be here in about an hour. We're supposed to keep the whale wet," I told Stephanie. "Can you drive the golf cart back to the apartment and get some towels?"

She hesitated, and I knew she was going to say she'd never driven a golf cart before. "Listen, it's easy. Just press down on the gas and steer."

Stephanie got back on the golf cart, tentatively pushed on the gas, and headed off slowly. While she was gone, I took the bucket down to the surf again and again, filling it and bringing it back and pouring it gently over the whale's skin. The freezing water sloshed on my hands and pants and coat. After a lot of trips, I was out of breath and had to sit down next to the whale's head to rest. I touched his large, smooth forehead.

"We're working on it, Nick, buddy," I told the whale. "I don't know how we're going to get you back in the water." I gazed into his large sad eye as I spoke. The winter wind whistled as it blew over us. "But we're going to try."

Nick blinked. How long could Nick live out of the water? As if reading my thoughts, he gave another squeaking call that almost sounded like he was saying, "Help." The high-pitched call sounded like it came from a tiny bird, not a twelve-foot whale. And then he made a series of soft clicks.

My throat began to throb. What must it be like for him, to be stuck on land like this? As fast as he could swim in his world, in the water, he was completely helpless on land. And the calls and clicks. Was he trying to communicate with the rest of the whales in his group? I looked out to sea, straining to see a glimpse of fins that would show that the rest of his group was out there waiting and looking for him. I imagined being able to drag him back into the water. I imagined him leaping from the waves with gratitude, then swimming away to freedom, to rejoin his group.

If I saw this whale out in the water while I was swimming, I probably would be terrified. But out of his element, Nick was weak, barely able to move.

The wind blew and I shivered. Since I'd been down here, no one had walked by. My fingers were so red, raw, and cold from dumping water on Nick that I couldn't feel them. I balled up my hands and hugged them under my arms. The wet from the sand was seeping through my jeans.

I looked again into the whale's wise and kindly eye. I thought I could see his suffering. Was he in pain? As if in answer, he gave a quick, rushing breath. I thought my heart would burst.

Then Stephanie and Mom screeched to a stop in the golf cart and jumped down. A pile of towels lay behind them in the golf-bag storage area.

"I can't believe the whale is back up here!" Mom cried. "I wonder what's wrong?" She grabbed the pile of towels and handed some to me and some to Stephanie. "Let's get these wet, so we can lay them over it."

We ran down to the water and dunked the towels. My running shoes sank into the soft sand and then a freezing wave snaked over them, getting my feet wet. We carried the dripping, heavy towels back up the beach and carefully spread them over the rubbery skin of the whale.

I thought I heard the whale sigh. The sound of that sigh tore through me.

"Let's go inside now," Mom said. "It's freezing out here."

"No! I'm not leaving Nick!"

"Diana, you told them where the whale was, didn't you? They'll have no trouble finding it. They know what to do."

"No, I'm staying here. She told me to pour water over him! I'm going to keep doing that until they get here!" I grabbed the shell bucket and ran back down to the edge of the water. I filled the bucket and lugged it back up and then poured it gently over Nick's head. Then I went back down to the water and filled it again. I had to do something. This was something I could do. Again and again, ignoring Mom's pleas to stop, I filled the bucket and poured water over Nick, until I had soaked the whale from head to tail.

Finally, I sat down again in the sand beside Nick's head. The wind was making my eyes tear, and my hands and arms were red and cold. I was shivering violently. But I didn't care.

Mom had a few big, dry beach towels, and she came and wrapped one around me, one around Stephanie, and then sat down close to me. Stephanie came and sat next to Mom.

Again, the whale sighed.

"It's hard to watch a creature suffering like this, isn't it?" Mom said.

"Why do things like this happen? This is why I don't believe in God," I said. I remembered that night last spring, sitting in the sea grass with Cody, watching the mare and her foal on the beach. The mare had been injured and in terrible pain. It was almost intolerable to watch. Tears came to my eyes as I remembered.

"We don't know why this whale beached itself," Mom said. "But I know what you mean. Last night, when we were in the hospital talking with Grammy, I was thinking about how much pain Grammy was in and how hard it was to see that."

"I wanted to leave," I said.

Suddenly Stephanie got up and, without a word, walked away from us until she was out of earshot. She stood, facing away from us, the towel wrapped tightly around her.

"I wonder if we upset Stephanie with our conversation," Mom said, looking after her. "I'm glad that you want to stay and help the whale," Mom went on. "We need to be like that for Grammy too. We need to be strong enough."

I didn't want to talk about this anymore. Mom had been listening to Dr. Shrink too much. And what was the deal with Stephanie?

Suddenly, a police car and an old white truck appeared down the beach. They got closer and closer and stopped a few yards away from Nick. Three men and a woman, all wearing bright-orange weatherproof suits, jumped out of the back of the truck and headed toward us. One of the guys looked around our age. Both cab doors slammed as a man and a woman climbed out. That man, who had a gray beard, gave a whistle as he approached Nick.

Nick moved his head slightly, then whistled faintly back.

"That's encouraging. The animal is responsive," said the man.

"Oh, yeah," I said, anxious for them to know what good shape Nick was in. "He's been breathing and whistling and moving his tail and everything. We've been keeping him wet, like we were told."

"Great," said the man. "Thanks for calling us, and thanks for doing such a good job keeping the whale wet with the towels. I'm Dr. Eric Leland from the Marine Mammal Stranding Network." He held out his hand, and Mom and Stephanie and I all shook it. Then he introduced the others who were there. "Most of us are marine mammal researchers, and we volunteer for the network. And this is Dr. Bob Cohn, our veterinarian." He pointed to a stocky guy with a beard and mustache, who nodded and said, "Hi."

Dr. Leland turned to his colleagues. "Looks like a short-finned pilot, a year or two old. The whale is breathing, making echolocations, and moving his flukes. But the animal is in poor body condition. It looks emaciated."

"This is the second time Nick's stranded himself," I said. "We already pushed him back in the water once today."

"Really?" Dr. Leland said, giving me a closer look.

"Yes," said Mom. "It was about a quarter of a mile that way down the beach. My daughter and some surfers were able to push it back out to sea. Why would it strand itself a second time?"

"We don't know for sure," Dr. Leland said. "We do know that animals sometimes strand themselves when they are sick or injured."

"He has a nick on his top fin," I said. "That's why I named him Nick."

"When we study wildlife, we don't normally give animals names," said Dr. Leland. "Anyway, that's an old injury to the dorsal fin. It has nothing to do with what's happening today. It could mean this guy survived a shark attack or something."

"Really?" I said. Surviving a shark attack! Imagine!

Dr. Leland shrugged. "Maybe." The group gathered around the whale's head, discussing the breathing sounds and the whistling. A cold afternoon wind picked up, and a cloud moved in front of the sun.

"It's going to be dark in a couple of hours," Dr. Leland told the others.

"Let's go ahead and get some blood," said Dr. Cohn. He went to the truck and came back with a syringe, and some test tubes. He and one of the volunteers went to Nick's tail. He felt around on the tail fin until he found a spot that satisfied him, then he inserted the needle. Soon dark blood snaked up the plastic tubing, and Dr. Cohn began filling the test tubes with it.

The boy our age came and stood beside us. He was thin, with pale, freckled skin, expressive greenish eyes, and red hair.

"Why do they take blood?" I asked him.

"They'll use that iSTAT machine to analyze it." The boy pointed to a machine that Dr. Cohn was holding. It looked like a large white television remote with a small screen at the top and a panel of buttons down below. "They'll be able to tell the condition of the whale, like if it's sick. I'm Jeremy, by the way. I'm a volunteer."

"Hey. I'm Diana." Then, I asked, "How long will that take?"

"Just a coupla minutes," said Jeremy. "It'll show if there are really bad health problems."

My heart leaped to my throat. "What do you mean, 'really bad health problems'? You guys are going to save Nick, aren't you?"

"Sure, if we can," Jeremy said. "It's just that usually whales don't beach themselves unless there's something really wrong." He and the others headed back toward the truck, where they unloaded a large blue stretcher and brought it over beside Nick. All working together, the group rolled Nick to the right and slid the stretcher underneath him. Then they walked to the other side, rolled Nick to the left, and pulled the stretcher the rest of the way under so that he was completely restrained on the stretcher. He blew out breath and flicked his tail weakly.

I got as close as I could to Nick's head. I watched his big, sad eye. Some grains of sand were stuck on his eye, and I reached over to brush them away.

"Diana, come wait over here with me," Mom said.

"But he has sand in his eye!" I said. "I want to get it out!"

I took a few reluctant steps away from Nick. "Do you need me to pour more water on him?" I asked Dr. Leland.

"Sure, but just stay near the head. Don't get too close to the flukes," Dr. Leland said. "You never know what can happen with those."

I grabbed the bucket and raced down toward the water. The tide had gone out, and it was a long walk. Just seeing all these people surrounding Nick was upsetting me. I had a terrible feeling.

While I was getting the water, I looked out to sea, again searching for a group of fins, weaving back and forth out in the water. Was Nick's family out there waiting for him? My heart started to beat faster, and I raced back with the bucket of water. Nick was suspended on the stretcher, his fins wrapped close to his body. The stranding crew stood watching Nick now, their arms crossed over their chests, talking in low voices. His blowhole opened, and he blew a rapid breath, and then gave a thin bird-like call.

I darted forward and gently poured a stream of water over Nick's head, then sat down near Jeremy, watching Nick's eye.

Meanwhile, Dr. Cohn was looking at the screen of the iSTAT machine. Dr. Leland joined him, looking over his shoulder.

"There are electrolyte changes and indications of shock," Dr. Cohn said. "This animal is in acidosis. It's also dehydrated."

Why weren't they in more of a hurry to get Nick back in the water? I couldn't understand what was going on. Were they planning to send Nick to a rehabilitation facility? Some of the nature shows I'd seen had dolphins that had been saved and sent to places like that.

Just then, Mom came up and knelt beside me. "Diana, Stephanie and I are going to go back to the apartment. We need to be home in time for hospital visiting hours."

"No, I can't leave! I have to stay here!" I turned away from Mom and again looked into Nick's watery eye.

"Is it all right if she stays?" Mom asked Dr. Leland.

"It's fine," he said.

Mom squeezed my shoulder and looked at her watch. "All right. You need to head home in about thirty more minutes. You can find your way back?"

I nodded, and a minute or so later I heard the golf cart drive away.

Dr. Leland came and sat beside me by Nick's head with a clipboard. Every time Nick took a breath, he'd check the second hand on his watch and make a note. "Shallow breathing," he said to Dr. Cohn.

"Why aren't you putting Nick back into the water?" I asked.

"Several reasons," Dr. Leland said. "First of all, this is a short-finned pilot whale. This species lives fifty miles offshore. Also, they're a social species, they live in matriarchal groups. Just pushing a pilot whale back into the water here isn't going to do it any good. Here it would be out of its habitat, away from its pod."

"So it can't live away from its family?"

"No, not alone like this," Dr. Leland said. "We've also gotten a lot of signs that this animal isn't in good condition. It's emaciated; it's not very active. And look, we're able to touch and stroke it. Any time you can touch a wild animal, something is terribly wrong."

My heart squeezed. I blinked.

Nick took another breath, and Dr. Leland looked at his watch and made another notation.

"Its breaths are shallow. Not deep the way we'd like it. Every minute that goes by, the whale's systems are breaking down."

I could hardly talk. I felt rising panic. "But what can we do? We have to do something! We have to save him!"

"Sometimes you can't save them," Dr. Leland said, looking at me kindly. "We'll stay here with it. We'll try and keep the scene very quiet and stress free for it. You're welcome to stay here with us."

Nick took another breath, Dr. Leland checked his watch and made a note. I realized it had been awhile since Nick had moved his tail. I looked at his wrinkled eye again.

He blinked slowly. Dr. Leland sighed. A lump formed in my throat.

"Why don't you name animals?" I asked him, starting to understand.

"Because we want to try to remain objective," he said, clearing his throat. "Wild animals aren't pets. We can't protect animals from what happens in the wild. We don't want to interfere. We just want to respect and learn about them."

"But I'm not sorry I pushed him back in the water

today. I thought I was doing the right thing," I whispered.

"Pushing him back in the water was like someone coming to an emergency room and the doctors sending them away, saying, 'Heal thyself.' But it's okay. You didn't know. If we'd been here, we would have told you not to do it," Dr. Leland said.

Nick drew a shallow breath. He gave a faint cry that made my throat ache. His tail twitched. Dr. Leland made a note of it.

Members of the stranding crew sat quietly around Nick now. No one was talking. Jeremy, sitting next to me, ran his hand down Nick's side gently.

The pounding of the surf behind me was harsh and endless, unstopping, and the wind buffeted my ears. Tears swelled in my eyes, streamed down my cheeks.

Nick drew one last breath.

A white bird flew over us.

And Nick stopped moving.

12

STEPHANIE

When Lynn and I got back to Grammy's apartment, Jelly came bounding on his fat, little legs to the door, barking, but then, when he saw it was us, he moped back to Grammy's room. Then he crawled under Grammy's bed.

"Just look at that poor dog," Lynn said.

Daddy sat at the kitchen counter, on the computer, catching up with work and listening to Jackson Browne on his iPod. As we were taking off our coats and gloves, Jackson sang about being out walking and not doing much talking these days.

For some reason, those words made me think about how Daddy must feel with his mother sick. Lynn went and wrapped her arms around his neck and gave him a kiss on the forehead. He looked up. "Well?" he said. "Where's Diana? She knows we need to go to the hospital later."

"I give you a kiss, and that's all you have to say?" said Lynn.

Daddy had been more impatient with all of us, especially Diana, since Grammy had gotten sick. But I was more impatient with her too.

"We still have plenty of time before visiting hours start," Lynn said. "Diana was captivated by the situation with the whale, and I thought it was all right to let her stay."

"I wish you had made her come back," Daddy said. "I don't want her holding us up."

"Norm, I'll make sure she doesn't," Lynn said shortly, and then headed into the kitchen. Dishes clattered as she began to unload the dishwasher.

Daddy got up from the computer and started helping her, putting away the silverware. "We need to remember Grammy is the reason we're here."

"I do! But we can't spend every minute at the hospital. They have visiting hours for a reason."

"My family never paid attention to visiting hours," Daddy said, shutting the silverware drawer. "We go there and we stay."

"It's families like yours that drive the medical staff nuts." Lynn slammed a cabinet door. "Your mother will get worn out with us sitting there 24/7."

"How do you know how my mother feels?"

My heart started pounding. Was a fight starting? Daddy and Lynn didn't usually fight the way Daddy and Mama had. Memories of Daddy and Mama fighting started racing through my head. Blocking out the rise of their voices, I went back to my bedroom, shut the door, and found my sketchpad. I tried to work on my drawing of the conch shell arrangement. The light had changed since this morning, and the shadow beside the shells had grown and deepened. My mind kept jumping to different memories, and I couldn't concentrate.

It had been sad and scary out there watching the crew with the whale. I didn't know why they hadn't tried to push the whale back into the water. The longer I'd stayed, the harder it was to listen to the whale's breathing as it got shallower and shallower. I was glad we'd left. But why had the whale stranded itself? I still didn't understand.

I checked my phone. Colleen had texted to tell

me that Andy ("Panda Eyes") had texted her. When I read that, in the middle of all that was happening with my family, I felt like texting back, "Who cares?" But I didn't. I knew she was excited, so I texted back, "Great!" And Noah had texted me again. He had started telling me that he understood about having a sick grandparent and about what happened when he'd gone to Richmond for his grandfather's heart bypass surgery. He said his whole family had slept in the waiting room, because his grandfather wasn't allowed to have visitors the first day.

Daddy and Lynn's voices had stopped. Light was starting to fade now. I hoped Diana got back soon.

Lynn had actually just put on her coat to go look for Diana when she walked in the door. The minute I saw Diana's face I knew.

"Did it …?"

She sat down on the couch and began to bawl. Big, heaving, heartbreaking sobs. I couldn't help it. I started to cry too.

"I'm sorry, Diana." Lynn went over and rubbed her shaking shoulders. Her coat was halfway wet again and her jeans were covered with wet sand.

"Sometimes those things just happen, sweetie," Lynn said. "Nature can be harsh."

"Jeremy said we helped him have a good death," Diana cried. "They're going to examine the body to see if they can find out what was wrong. Dr. Leland said I can call tomorrow to find out."

Diana curled in her mother's arms, crying. I wiped tears from my own cheeks. I thought about the meaning of those words, "a good death." I didn't know what that meant.

On the way over to the hospital, we were quiet. A pall hung over us. When we got into Grammy's room and gathered around her bed, she immediately asked what was wrong.

"You girls look like you've been crying," she said. I thought she was sitting up a little straighter and had a bit more color in her face. We told her what had happened to the whale.

"I kept wondering why they didn't put Nick back in the water," Diana said.

"I'm so sorry that happened," Grammy said. "We really become so attached to animals, don't we? I don't know what I'd do if something happened to Jelly. I just wish I could see him," she said. "I worry about him. He's used to being with me."

"He's doing fine, Mom," Daddy assured her.

"He doesn't like me," Diana told Grammy. "I've never had a dog not like me. It hurts my feelings. I know you said for me to take care of him, but I can't, because he won't have anything to do with me."

"Isn't that the funniest thing?" Grammy said. "I would have never guessed that."

"I'm taking care of him for you, Angela," Lynn said. "We took him out on the beach today. But he does miss you. Every time someone comes to the door, Jelly runs to greet them, thinking it's you. Then he's so disappointed that it's not."

"I talk to him all the time," said Grammy. She pulled the covers up around her tighter. "He's a good listener."

An attendant passed in the hallway, pushing a cart stacked with trays of food. The smell of turkey and yeast rolls floated into the room.

"I wish I could have something to eat," said Grammy.

"I'm afraid you'll have to wait on that," Daddy said. "It shouldn't be too much longer."

Dr. Claiborne stopped in. She looked at Grammy's chart, then looked at Grammy and smiled. "Good news!" she said. "The pancreatitis is clearing up."

"Yay!" Lynn and Daddy said.

I felt relief wash over me like a shower of warm water. "So Grammy is going to be okay?" I blurted out.

Dr. Claiborne grinned. "You've been pretty anxious,

haven't you? Well, we're encouraged by your grand-mother's progress." She turned toward Grammy. "What I'd like to do is schedule you for gallbladder surgery three days from now."

"Three days?"

"While the pancreas is quiet, yes. To get it over with. We have a window of opportunity we should take advantage of."

"What does the surgery involve?" Daddy asked.

Dr. Claiborne described the way the surgeon would make three small incisions in Grammy's abdomen and insert a surgical device that would extract the gallbladder.

"The surgeon will come by tomorrow morning to talk with you about it."

Lynn patted Grammy's arm. "I had a patient who had that done just a few weeks ago. She went home from the hospital the next day," she assured Grammy.

Before we left, I gave Grammy a big hug. Her arms, wrapped around me, felt light but substantial. I skipped across the room and did a twirl on the way out the door.

Everything was going to be okay!

While we were in the elevator I suddenly remem-bered my prayer, asking God please not to let Grammy die. Now she was better. Had God answered my prayer? Goosebumps prickled the back of my neck. Maybe God had. I felt a lightness, like warm sun shining on my face, and a sense of peace traveled through my whole body.

"How about we go out to eat?" Daddy said as we climbed into the car. "To celebrate Grammy's progress."

"Yay!" I said.

"Great idea," said Lynn.

Diana didn't say anything.

We went to one of Grammy's favorite fish restaurants in Morehead City, a place Daddy and I almost always went when we were here with Grammy, but Diana and Lynn hadn't ever been to.

"This restaurant started in the 1930s as a fresh fish market. Pretty soon the owners installed a few stools for people to eat, and now it's one of the biggest seafood restaurants around," Daddy said.

In the waiting room, black-and-white photographs from decades ago covered the walls. There were two big rooms, each lined with long wooden tables. They served all kinds of fried seafood, hush puppies, and coleslaw, and they had a gift shop with their famous saltwater taffy in the front. Through the window beside our table, we could see boats moored to the dock outside. Even though it was dark, an occasional boat with lights went by.

The server brought a basket of steaming hush puppies. It seemed that visiting the hospital had left us starved. We grabbed for them. Before I knew it, I had eaten three.

"I wish Grammy could be here with us," Daddy said. "She loves this place!"

"She can't even eat real food yet," I said.

Diana, quiet, watched a boat with lights slide by, creating shifting flashes on the choppy dark water as it passed. I knew she was thinking about the whale.

"We'll bring her next time," Lynn said. "Meanwhile, here's a toast to Grammy's health!"

We toasted with our water glasses.

After all the worry over Grammy, we all felt tired and giddy. I ordered a fried-shrimp basket, which is what I always got when we went there. Diana didn't feel like eating anything but a salad. Daddy and Lynn split a broiled flounder platter. When our food came, we ate like we hadn't eaten in days.

When we arrived back at Grammy's apartment, Jelly didn't come to the door to greet us. Calling him, we headed down the hall to Grammy's bedroom and found him wedged under the bed with his nose nestled between his front paws, his brown eyes glinting with distrust there in the dark.

"Jelly, what are you doing under there?" Lynn said, peeking under the bed skirt. She sat back on her heels. "Do you think dogs can get depressed?"

"Of course," Diana said.

"I guess so," I said.

"Oh, come on," said Daddy.

Later that night, Diana and I lay in the twin beds with the lights off. She had been terribly quiet since the whale died. I was so happy about Grammy that I felt forgiving toward Diana for how she had acted and felt like opening up to her again.

"Are you okay?" I asked. A band of light from the living room outlined the door, and we could hear the rise and fall of Daddy and Lynn's voices as they discussed how long we could stay after Grammy got home from the hospital. Lynn was worried about taking too many days off work.

"Have you seen many things die?" Diana asked.

"No," I said honestly. "Have you?"

"One time, when I was about eight, I was out in the yard of our old house, and I heard these birds making a really loud racket. They were dive-bombing one of the bushes beside the house. It was all kinds of birds—robins and bluebirds and brown ones and one with a black head. They were all squawking and flying at this bush."

"Weird."

"Yeah. So I went over to the bush to see what was there, and I saw a black snake curled around a bird's nest with baby birds in it. It was eating the baby birds."

I gasped. "That's awful!"

"I know. I got so scared. It was kind of dark in the bush, and I could just barely see the outline of the snake. Meanwhile the birds kept flying around, dive-bombing the snake and squawking at it. I thought, *Those birds are so small compared to the snake, but they're attacking it. And I'm so much bigger than the snake.* I went inside and got a broom and tried to sweep the snake out of the bush, but it was wrapped too tightly around the branches."

"I can't believe you tried to sweep that snake out of the bush! What if the snake had bitten you, Diana? I would have gotten out of there as fast as I could."

"But I thought I should try to be as brave as the birds. They were trying to fight the snake. Then Mom came out and made me put the broom away and go inside. The next day I saw the empty nest, and I cried for like an hour, I was so mad. Those poor little baby birds. Sometimes I have dreams about that scene."

I shuddered. "I would too. That sounds horrible."

"Seeing Nick die today was like that. A scene I won't ever forget. I felt so helpless. The way his breathing just got shallower and shallower, and then it stopped, and he stopped moving. I don't understand why he stranded himself, I don't understand why he died. I don't know. It makes me think that the world is a terrible place when things like that can happen. I mean, how could God let Nick die? How could God let those baby birds die?"

I didn't know how to answer Diana's question. "I don't know, Diana. But with the baby birds ... Isn't it like a miracle that the birds all banded together to fight the snake, even though they were so much smaller? And with Nick ... you and the other people were around Nick to comfort him when he died. Like Jeremy said, he had a good death."

Diana was quiet for a minute. "Oh," she finally said. "You're saying that the bad things happening inspired other living things to help."

"Yeah, I guess. And I guess I think of that as being where God comes in."

She was silent for a minute or so. She turned over in her bed to face me, pulling her covers to her chin. "That guy Jeremy, the high school kid, came and sat with me and talked to me for a while after it happened. He tried to comfort me. He was nice."

"He did seem nice," I said. "Cool red hair."

I wanted, then, to talk to Diana about praying for Grammy not to die, and wondering if God had answered my prayer. But I didn't say anything. She probably wouldn't believe me. She would probably say Grammy just got better because of the doctors. Maybe it was just something that I had to search my heart about.

While we were having breakfast the next morning, Diana asked Lynn if she could have her phone back. "Dr. Leland said I could call today to see if they found out what caused Nick to die. Can I have my phone back so I can call him?"

Lynn looked at Diana thoughtfully, glanced at Daddy, then reached in her purse and handed Diana the phone her dad had given her. "I guess I've made my point," Lynn said.

Diana pulled a scrap of paper out of her pocket and tapped in the numbers, walking away from us. "Hi, Dr. Leland?" she said, looking out the window at the golf cart. "This is Diana from the beach yesterday. You said I could call you today to see if you found out why the whale died." She listened for a few seconds, then said, "Okay, I'll call back later. Thanks." She hung up and held the phone in her lap. "He said they're getting ready to do the necropsy now. He says to call back in a few hours."

Since Grammy was doing so much better, Lynn

talked Daddy into skipping morning visiting hours and going to downtown Beaufort. Beaufort was a historic waterfront town more than two hundred years old. Daddy said he'd heard that the town hadn't changed much since it was built in the 1700s. It was said, he added, that the brutal pirate Blackbeard was a frequent visitor in Beaufort when he needed to resupply. We walked down Front Street, where small, white clapboard houses with columned porches and historical markers by their front doors looked out on the water. A few blocks down, in between a waterfront restaurant and a line of shops, was a marina where gleaming yachts and slim sailboats with shiny teak decks and neatly furled sails bobbed by the docks.

A block farther down and across the street was the Maritime Museum. It was a small, nautical-looking building with gray cedar shingles and painted white trim. I had been there once before with Grammy but couldn't remember very much about it. We walked in and who should we see but Jeremy, Diana's friend from yesterday.

"Jeremy!" Diana went over to him. He was wearing khakis and a black T-shirt with a white whale skeleton on the front, and he had a nametag that said Volunteer.

"Hey!" he said. I know Diana would say that I was reading too much into things, but I promise that his face lit up when he saw her. "Diana, right?"

"Yeah. And you remember my stepsister, Stephanie?"

I headed over, and we said "Hi" to each other.

Diana pointed at Jeremy's nametag. "So you're a volunteer?"

"Yeah. I helped put together that whale skeleton." The skeleton, enormous and gleaming white with a pointed-looking jaw, hung from the ceiling, arching over the rest of the whale exhibit. "It's over thirty-three feet long. Guess how much its heart weighed?"

"How much?" Diana asked.

"One hundred and fifteen pounds."

"Wow."

"The whale stranded itself on Cape Lookout a couple of years ago, out near where the lighthouse is. After it died, the museum staff buried the whale and waited a few years, then dug it up and reassembled the skeleton."

We were all silent, thinking about Nick. Diana blinked a few times, then asked, "Why did that whale die?"

Jeremy shrugged. "It was a total mystery. They did a necropsy but never found out."

"They're doing a necropsy on Nick today."

"Yeah, I wanted to go but couldn't, because I had already committed to work here today. It will be good to find out what was wrong with him."

"So you volunteer for both the Marine Mammal Stranding Network and for the museum?" I said.

"Yeah," Jeremy said. "I'm going to apply to go to UNC Wilmington in their marine sciences department."

"What year in school are you?" Diana asked.

"I'm a sophomore."

"We're freshmen."

Just then Daddy and Lynn, who had been signing the guest book and making a donation, came over. Diana introduced them.

"Hey, listen, do you want me to show you around?" Jeremy asked.

He took us straight to a big display on whaling in the center of the museum. He described how, a hundred or so years ago, on the coast of North Carolina, men would camp on the shore with a lookout who spotted migrating whales that were passing by. They would follow the whales in small boats and fire at them with harpoons or whale guns. Jeremy explained that they hunted the whales for their oil to use in oil lamps and also for their baleen.

"What's baleen?" Diana asked.

"Baleen is flexible strands of keratin that a lot of whales have instead of teeth," Jeremy explained. "It's the same stuff as your fingernails. They use it to filter tiny fish, like krill."

"Did Nick have baleen?" I asked.

"No, he had teeth," Diana said. "I saw them."

"Right," said Jeremy. "Pilot whales have teeth."

"What was the baleen used for?" Daddy asked.

"It was used to make something for women's clothing," said Jeremy.

"This display says it was used for stays in women's corsets," Lynn said. "And—can you believe it—it says whale hunting basically stopped when corsets went out of style. That's amazing. I thought it was all about the oil. But it was about fashion!"

"And you know how we were talking yesterday about why researchers don't name the whales and dolphins that they study?" Jeremy said to Diana. "Well, one thing that was unusual about the North Carolina whalers was that they did name their whales. There was a famous whale named Mayflower that dragged one boat eight miles out to sea before it finally died."

"Eight miles!" Diana said.

"And back here, it's really cool," said Jeremy. "We've got artifacts from Blackbeard's ship, the *Queen Anne's Revenge*! People had been looking for that ship for years, and they finally found it not very far from here, in really shallow water in Bogue Banks. The water was only about twenty-five feet deep. There's also a great video about the excavation of the site."

Jeremy and Diana got ahead of the rest of us. I could tell by the way Jeremy was focusing on her as he talked that he was into her. I couldn't wait to talk to her about it. She probably didn't even realize it! I watched them as they strolled by the things on display that the pirates had used—bottles, pieces of stoneware, and glass beads used for trading. Pieces of the ship, like rigging hooks, a bilge pump sieve, and pieces of sailcloth, were also displayed.

I hung back with Daddy and Lynn. She was interested in the physicians' tools that were on display. But most of what was displayed was weapons and ammunition. There were cannons, cannonballs, rifles, swords, pistols and knives by the dozens.

"Looks like all these pirates did was fight," Daddy said, as we filed past the glass cases holding the lavish weapons display.

"Blackbeard had a gruesome reputation," Lynn said. Drawings of Blackbeard portrayed him as a fierce-looking man with burning candles embedded in his long black beard.

At the back of the museum, we watched an interesting video showing how divers worked on different quadrants of the Queen Anne's Revenge wreck site to recover artifacts.

As we headed back to the front, passing by the different examples of fishing boats, like flatbottom skiffs and sharpies, and displays about the lighthouses on the North Carolina coast, I glanced over at Diana and Jeremy. She was laughing at something he'd said.

"Look at this," Daddy said. "The lighthouse keepers' wife and children usually lived on the mainland during the winter so they could go to school, and they would just join their father at the lighthouse during the summer."

Lynn poked me with her elbow. "Are you checking that out?" she said quietly, inclining her head toward Diana and Jeremy.

"Yep," I said. "Sure am."

We smiled at each other.

"What are you two smiling about?" Daddy said, as he joined us back at the entrance.

"Oh, nothing," Lynn teased. "Men are so oblivious, aren't they, Stephanie?" She reached over and pinched Daddy's cheek.

Daddy knitted his brows and looked from Lynn to me and back to Lynn.

"What's taking Diana so long?"

"That's what we're smiling about," I said.

13

DIANA

I could see Stephanie, Mom, and Norm standing outside the museum waiting for me. "Well," I said to Jeremy. "Thanks for showing us around. It was great running into you."

"Hey," said Jeremy. "Don't leave yet. Let's call Dr. Leland now." He got out his cell phone and tapped in the number. He held the phone close to my ear so we could both listen when Dr. Leland answered.

His curly red hair tickled my temple, and I got a slight tingle down my spine. When Dr. Leland answered, Jeremy's hand, which was on the phone, touched my ear. My heart thudded. I felt funny, standing so close. I usually like my space.

"Yes, Jeremy," came Dr. Leland's voice. "We did finish the necropsy a few minutes ago. That pilot whale had unfortunately swallowed several plastic bags and other pieces of plastic that had abraded its stomach. The plastic bags were preventing it from getting nutrition. It starved to death."

"Starved to death?" I drew in my breath and tears started to my eyes. I told myself not to cry in front of Jeremy. Poor Nick!

"Yes," Dr. Leland continued, "it's a very unfortunate result of people throwing trash into the ocean. To a young whale, a plastic bag looks a lot like a squid, its favorite food."

Jeremy talked to Dr. Leland for a minute more, then thanked him and hung up. I rubbed my coat sleeve across my cheek. That poor whale! I thought again about being out there on the beach, with the sound of the wind and the waves, listening to Nick breathe his last. My heart pounded. I didn't want Nick to have died for no reason. I wanted to do something to help.

"Hey," Jeremy said, peering at me closely. "Are you okay?"

"I'm just thinking again about him dying, that's all."

"I know. Since I've been a volunteer, I've seen it happen a couple of times. In fact, there's only been one dolphin that was in good enough shape to send to rehab. It's terrible, but most of the time they don't make it."

"I just didn't know. It's so sad."

Jeremy put his phone in his pocket. "Well, you know, I've learned that animals strand themselves for a reason. Maybe we don't know that something's wrong, but they do. Anyway, you seem like you need cheering up. I'm off from the museum in fifteen minutes. Want to walk around Beaufort and hang out on the docks?"

I stared at Jeremy and all his freckles. I held back an impulse to turn around and see if he was talking to someone standing behind me. Did Jeremy like me or something? I didn't get it. He was really being nice. Hanging out on the docks would be pretty cool. After a second I said, "Let me ask." I ran outside to where Mom and Norm and Stephanie were waiting. "Jeremy invited me to hang out and walk around Beaufort this afternoon," I said.

I scanned Mom's and Norm's faces. Did I want them to say yes? Then again, maybe they'd say no. Part of me was scared to be with Jeremy all afternoon. Maybe it would be better if they said no.

"Well—" Mom said. She looked like she was considering it.

Norm checked his watch. "Visiting hours start at four."

I knew it! He was going to say no! My heart was beating a tattoo on the inside of my ribs. I didn't know what I wanted them to say!

Mom put her hand on Norm's arm. "Norm, let's talk about this." She walked away from us and beckoned to him. They stood together, whispering to each other, their backs to us. But I clearly heard Mom say, "You and I need a little time together."

"Looks like Lynn is trying to talk Daddy into it," Stephanie said, poking me with her elbow and raising her eyebrows. "You know Jeremy is into you, don't you, Diana?

"If they say yes, come with us," I said impulsively. "I want to hang out with him but not by myself."

Stephanie glanced at Jeremy through the museum door.

"Don't look at him! He'll know we're talking about him!"

He waved at us, smiling. Stephanie waved back.

"Oh, I'm so embarrassed!" I said. I could feel my face turning hot.

Meanwhile, Mom and Norm rejoined us.

"Diana, your mom and I have discussed this."

There they went again. Mom letting Norm decide and then announce it like he's in charge.

"Wait," I said. "If I go, Stephanie's coming too. It's not just me." That might fit in with them needing a little time together too.

Norm and Mom exchanged a look, and Mom nodded at him. "Jeremy seems like a nice young man," he said. "You girls are welcome to go get some lunch and walk around Beaufort with him and look at the shops and boats at the marina while the two of us go to lunch together. We'll meet you back at the car in three hours, in time to go to the hospital for visiting hours this afternoon. Sound fair?"

Stephanie and I looked at each other in surprise, laughing.

"Sounds great!" Stephanie said.

Norm put his arm around Mom, grinning. "Hey, we get to have a romantic lunch together. We've had a lot of togetherness in Grammy's little apartment. So we're getting something out of this too!"

"Well, Diana?" Stephanie said, giving me a little shove. "Don't just stand there. Go tell him we can go!"

Ten minutes later, we were walking along the marina with Jeremy. I looked at his fluffy red hair and cute freckles and pinched myself. A boy liked me, not Stephanie! Here we were on a sunny winter day, walking along a boat dock, not down a hospital corridor. The water slapped soothingly and lazily against the dock pilings. There was no wind today, and in the sun, it was almost warm.

"The marina's pretty empty now, but you should see some of the boats that tie up here in the spring and summer," Jeremy was saying. He was skipping along backward, talking to us. "Fifty-foot yachts. People coming from the Bahamas and the Caribbean. People having drinks on the deck. A lot of decks made of teak," Jeremy said.

"Cool," said Stephanie.

We passed a small shopping area, a wooden boat works, a restaurant, and a dock area with signs advertising ferry rides.

"This place is hopping during the summer. Ferries run here most of the year," Jeremy explained.

"Where do the ferries go?" Stephanie asked.

"Oh ... out to where they found Blackbeard's ship. To the Cape Lookout Lighthouse. Or Shackleford Banks to see the wild horses."

My mouth dropped open. "Wild horses? I didn't know there were wild horses here!"

"Oh, yeah. They have their own little island," Jeremy said. "The only way you can see them is by boat."

I stood stock still. "You're kidding! I want to see the wild horses!"

Jeremy gave a shrug. "Well, there are no ferries running in the winter. But we could take our boat."

"What boat?" I caught my breath.

"My dad has a boat that we keep docked around the corner here," he said. "It's about twenty years old, and we've had to be towed in more than once, but I'll show you." He headed down the block, still talking. "We never did winterize it this year, because it's been so warm. I could take you to see the lighthouse, and then we could come back by Shackleford Banks."

A few blocks down, Jeremy led us to a small blue-and-white motorboat with a faded and patched boat cover. After Jeremy removed the cover, we saw that several of the seats had strips of silver duct tape covering small rips.

He jumped into the boat, pulled out a key with a little plastic floatie on it from his pocket, and turned on the motor. Then he plugged in his iPod. It was amazingly loud, coming from that broken-down boat. An oldie, "Listen to the Music," by the Doobie Brothers, came on with these opening guitar licks that made anybody listening want to dance.

"Hop in!" he said. He gave me his hand, and I hopped down into the boat, then turned to help Stephanie, who was standing on the dock with her arms crossed.

"C'mon!" I said. "We don't have to be back for three hours!"

"Daddy and Lynn didn't say anything about going out on a boat!" Stephanie said.

"They didn't say we couldn't!" I said. "It's wild horses, Steph! And a lighthouse!"

Stephanie didn't move. I realized she was scared of boats.

"Stephanie! Jeremy's a good boat driver, aren't you, Jeremy?"

"Yeah," Jeremy said. "My dad made me take the boat safety course."

Stephanie just stood on the dock, looking down at us with a doubtful expression on her face. "They thought we'd be walking around the town, not going out on a boat," Stephanie repeated. "I don't think we should go."

"Oh, Steph, come on," I said. As if she could tell that I was really starting to get irritated, she very slowly clambered down into the boat. It started rocking, and she grabbed my shoulder when she almost lost her balance. "We're going to get in trouble. I know it," she whispered to me.

"All right! We're all aboard! Diana, can you untie us?" Jeremy, at the wheel, pointed at the lines tied around the cleats at the dock.

"Sure." I unlooped the ropes from the cleats and dropped them into the boat.

Stephanie sat in the back, wrapping her scarf more tightly around her neck. "It's going to be freezing out on the water."

Jeremy, sitting on top of the driver's seat back, one foot on the floor and the other propped in the seat, slowly backed away from the dock. A few ducks scattered away from us. Then Jeremy engaged the throttle, the boat angled up in the water, and we headed out, the wind snatching phrases of the Doobie Brothers and carrying them across the water.

Jeremy and I sang along. Riding the waves in the boat felt fantastic, just like a horse cantering, and I went to the front, even though the wind was numbing, and sat on the bench-like seat that lined the bow. A small island was just to our right, and the Front Street houses, with their upstairs and downstairs porches, slid by on our left as Jeremy sped up, angling away from the coast.

"That's Carrot Island," Jeremy shouted over the wind, pointing at the island to our right.

"Wow! How long does it take to get to the lighthouse?" I shouted.

"About an hour," he shouted back. He cut across a

wave, and we crashed into the trough and spray flew up in my face. "Ha-ha! Sorry about that!" he said.

I sat with my legs stretched out along the bench as we cruised over the water, thinking how much this felt like riding a horse. Every day, the water was a slightly different color, and today it was greenish, with flashing sparkles from the sun. The sky was bright, but clouds were piling up against the horizon, and the winter sun shone with a grayish-yellow cast around the edges of the clouds. The driving beat from Fun.'s "We Are Young," talking about setting the world on fire, carried over the water. My cheeks were frozen, my hair whipped in the wind, and I plunged my hands into my coat pockets. Could I be any happier? I loved riding in boats! The faster the better!

I glanced back at Jeremy, his hands on the wheel, his red curls slicked back in the wind, and gave Stephanie, in the back, a thumbs-up. She gave me a shivering pantomime to show me how cold she was. Oh, she was driving me crazy.

We rode along and suddenly in the water I saw a dolphin, looping and swimming and diving beside us.

"Look!" I shouted at Jeremy, and pointed at the dolphin. His fin rose up and water shone on his rounded back.

"Yeah!" Jeremy shouted back. Breathless, I leaned

over and held my arm down toward the water to see if I could touch the dolphin. Freezing spray coated my arm. How deep was that water? I thought of Nick, about how this water had been his home.

A minute later, the dolphin peeled away from us and disappeared.

After awhile, I saw land on either side of us. We seemed to be heading up a channel. On a spit of land to our left rose a lighthouse.

"There's Cape Lookout!" Jeremy said, pointing ahead. "This is the most southern point of the Outer Banks."

As we approached the lighthouse, Jeremy slowed the boat. The wind died, and I stopped shivering. He tied up at one of several docks, and he and I clambered up onto the wooden slats.

"I don't think we should be doing this, but I'm not staying here by myself," Stephanie said as I reached down to help her climb up.

Just past a dune stood the lighthouse, painted in a black diamond pattern.

"Want to see if we can climb to the top?" Jeremy said. "Hey, did you know that each of the North Carolina lighthouses has a different pattern painted on it? Cape Lookout is black diamonds, Cape Hatteras has a black-and-white spiral. I forget the others."

We followed a wooden path over the sand past a visitors' center and the lightkeeper's house to the lighthouse. A sign said the lighthouse was closed for the winter, but there was a park ranger there and when Jeremy told him he worked for the Maritime Museum, he told us we could go up for fifteen minutes.

We went inside the dark lighthouse and started climbing the spiral stairs. They were steep, with tight curves, and a landing with a small window every couple of flights. Our voices and footsteps on the metal stairs echoed in the enclosed space. I quickly became warm from climbing and took my coat off.

"Y'all, don't leave me behind." Stephanie lagged far behind Jeremy and me. But we didn't wait.

We climbed and climbed from one landing to the next. The last flight of stairs was so steep it was like climbing a ladder. We were both panting when we finally reached the top. As I stepped out onto the metal catwalk, my heart pounded, my mouth went dry, and I got goose bumps. We were nearly two hundred feet in the air. Cold wind blew and buffeted against the supporting beams. There was a scrap of land far below us with some green vegetation, and a long thin strip of land to the north. To the south, the dunes tapered to a point. And in every other direction there was water, glittering, as far as we could see. Looking around at the view from the lighthouse, it almost seemed I could see far enough to see the curvature of the earth.

"See, there," said Jeremy, touching my shoulder. "That's Shackleford Banks, the island where the horses live. That's where we'll go next."

Shackleford Banks was off to the west, just past a short span of water, a pie-shaped tip attached to a long strip of land. Along the edge of the water, looking like toys, stood a group of tiny brown horses.

"Look!" I said to Jeremy.

"Yeah, so cool, right?"

"Y'all? Help!" We heard a small voice on the other side of the lighthouse. We followed the catwalk around and Stephanie was standing just outside the doorway on the catwalk, frozen, hanging onto the railing for dear life. "I can't move."

"What's the matter?" I said.

She could barely move her head to glance at me, and the look on her face showed sheer terror. "I can't look down. I can't move." Her face was white.

"Are you afraid of heights?" Jeremy asked.

"Apparently," she whispered.

"Okay," I said. I went over and took her hand. "Want me to take you back inside?"

She nodded, her eyes wide. Her fingers in mine were sweaty and shaking. I turned her around and led her over the ledge back through the door inside. She grabbed the railing with a gasp and almost collapsed.

"Are you going to be okay?" I asked.

She nodded wordlessly.

Jeremy and I skipped back to ground level, but I thought it was going to take Stephanie a half an hour to climb down, gripping the railing all the way. We thanked the park ranger and headed back to the dock.

"Shouldn't we go back now?" Stephanie said as she stepped carefully from the dock to the boat. But Jeremy and I ignored her.

"I can't wait to see the horses!" I yelled, as I jumped back into the boat. In a few minutes we were headed along the coast of Shackleford Banks.

"Shackleford Banks is nine miles long, and we've got to get to the other end, so we'll be riding along beside it for awhile," Jeremy yelled.

After awhile we finally reached the landing area. From the landing area point, the right side of the island looked like a sandy beach with breakers, the center of the island was grassy and treed, and the left side looked more like a bay, with its tide pools and vegetation. Standing right at the edge of the water on the bay side were about seven horses, bay and black, with long manes and tails and heavy winter coats, just like the ones I'd seen on the Outer Banks!

I stood up. "There they are!" I shouted.

"Sit down!" Jeremy shouted back, slowing the boat. "Don't stand up in the boat!"

Obediently, I sat back down but kept my eyes on the horses. As we approached, the horses raised their heads and pricked their ears at us, then began to run away, their tails sailing in the cold wind.

14

STEPHANIE

We were going to get in so much trouble. Why didn't I learn? Every time I did something with Diana she got me in trouble.

I was still feeling shaky from being up in the lighthouse. Diana had been nice to help me while I was up there, but now this boat bumping over the crests of the waves was scaring me to death, not to mention the fact that Jeremy was heading right for the beach, and I didn't see a dock anywhere.

"Where's the dock?" I shouted.

"No dock!" he shouted back. "I'm going to drive right up on the sand!"

Right up on the sand? Was he nuts?

I checked the digital clock on my phone. We were supposed to meet Daddy and Lynn back at the parking lot in less than an hour now. What if we didn't make it back in time?

Meanwhile Diana had her phone out and was taking pictures of the horses as they galloped away from us toward the bay side of the island.

"Go to the front so we don't have as much weight in the back," Jeremy yelled. I started to walk forward and just as I did, we dropped into a trough between two waves, and I fell to the floor of the boat.

"You okay?" Jeremy reached down and grabbed my arm to help me up.

I was so embarrassed! I scrambled up and headed to the front, sitting on the bench across from Diana. Jeremy cut the throttle to slow the boat as it nosed into shallower water, until at last we scraped bottom on the sand below us.

"We're here!" Jeremy cried, cutting the engine. "Somebody needs to jump off and push the boat a little higher up on the sand."

"You mean get wet?" I said. I had my new boots on!

Diana started laughing. "We'll do it. You stay in the boat until you can jump clear of the water." She stuck her phone in her sweatshirt pocket and jumped into the water, which was calf-deep. "Woooo! This will be the third time in two days I've had to wash my shoes."

"You mean that Lynn has had to wash your shoes," I pointed out.

Jeremy jumped into the water on the other side of the boat and together they pushed the boat, with me in it, partway up onto the sand.

At least now that the boat had stopped moving I wasn't so freezing cold.

I stood on the bow and both of them held their hands up so I could jump down. Well, here goes! I jumped, and they caught me as my boots sank in the wet sand. I followed at a walk as Jeremy and Diana raced across the beach toward the center of the island.

"What's here?" I yelled. It didn't look like much. Just sand and trees and sea grass. "Is there a bathroom or a place to get hot chocolate or anything?"

Jeremy started laughing. "Sorry, Stephanie. There's nothing on this island but horses. No shops."

I thought wistfully of the shops on Front Street that we could have spent the afternoon looking through. And we were supposed to have lunch. My stomach growled. All I wanted was to get back without getting into trouble.

"C'mon!" Diana shouted, skipping backward. "I want to get close to those horses!"

The horses had headed for the center of the island, which was higher ground with groves of twisty trees. We climbed over a dune and saw them grazing in a small meadow. Their winter coats were long and shaggy, and their tails almost dragged the ground. I finally caught up.

Diana slowed to a nonthreatening walk as she approached them. Close to us were two horses with reddish coats and light tails and manes, almost like palominos.

"How many horses are on this island?" Diana asked Jeremy.

"I don't know. Maybe a hundred?"

"And did these horses come from Spanish ships five hundred years ago, like the ones farther north in the Outer Banks?"

"Yeah, I think so," Jeremy said. "They've learned to dig holes with their hooves to drink the water here on the island. And they eat the sea grass."

"What happens to these horses if there's a hurricane?" I asked. "Do people come and round them up and take them to safety?"

"No, they just stay here," Jeremy said. "They find the high ground and huddle under the trees. I guess it's been that way for hundreds of years, and they've survived."

"Wow. They're so amazing," Diana said. "I found out when we saw the horses in the Outer Banks that you're not supposed to try to feed them or get too close. The stallions want to protect their mares and foals." She turned and grinned at us. "But wouldn't it be fantastic to ride one of these horses on the beach?"

"No!" I said.

"C'mon, let's explore!"

"We probably need to head back," I said, twisting my hair around one finger nervously. "We don't want to get in trouble. We don't want to be late."

"Oh, Stephanie, you're always worrying!" Diana said. "We just got here."

She headed in the direction of the horses, which were ambling along, slowly grazing their way across the meadow, their tails swishing rhythmically.

Diana and Jeremy weren't listening to me. They followed the horses and I, not knowing what else to do, tagged along behind. The afternoon wind picked up, stinging my eyes. I looked at the time on my phone again. How long would it take to drive the boat back?

And Grammy was there in her hospital bed, waiting

for us to come and visit her. If her healing was going well, she'd have surgery day after tomorrow.

I couldn't believe I had let myself get in another situation like this with Diana.

Meanwhile, I watched Diana and Jeremy together. He walked beside her, talking and waving his hands. Was she blind? Couldn't she see that he liked her?

I ran to catch up and caught the tail end of their conversation.

"So there was this young stallion, and I named him Firecracker," Diana was saying. "And I watched him get into a fight with the stallion that was the leader of his herd. Firecracker got thrown out of the herd."

"Oh, that must have been amazing," Jeremy said.

"Their fight was terrible to watch. Firecracker was standing off by himself, and every time he tried to walk closer, the black stallion charged him. And they'd rear up on their hind legs, and they were trying to pummel each other with their front hooves and bite each other's necks. And horses have to have the herd to survive. But by the end of our week there, Firecracker had found a friend. He'd found his own herd. It really gave me hope."

"Same way with the whales," Jeremy said. The wind blew his longish red bangs into his eyes, and he impatiently swiped them away. "They have to have their pod too. You know, pilot whales often follow one older female. Sometimes, if there's something wrong with the leader, she might strand herself, and then all the whales in the pod will follow her. So that's why whole groups of pilot whales sometimes strand themselves. And then, you know, it's such a tragedy, because they all die, but only one was sick."

Could two people be a better match? Listen to them talking about the lives of animals.

"I heard that sometimes sonar can cause whales to strand themselves," Diana said. "Is that true?" While she asked him this, she tiptoed to within a few feet of one of the horses that was grazing and kneeled to take a close-up picture of the horse's face and neck.

"I think the whales use echolocation to call to each other and, like, give each other directions. Some people say the sonar can mess them up. I heard about cases where entire pods of thirty whales have stranded themselves in shallow bays after the Navy did sonar testing."

"No kidding!" Diana said. She pointed at the horses that were grazing. "Look, see? The pinto is the stallion. All the other horses here are mares. And even though he's in the back of the herd, he's telling the mares which way to go. He directs them with his head."

Jeremy and I watched as the stallion did as Diana

described, lowering his head and slowly herding the mares along. Though the horses did not seem afraid of us, the stallion was slowly moving them away. Diana and Jeremy followed at a distance, still talking about animals. We came to the end of the pasture and started climbing a small dune. Just past the dune the horses began to melt into a grove of gnarled and twisted trees with shiny green leaves. The wind whistled through the gray, crooked branches.

"Oh, I almost forgot," Jeremy said. "Right out there is where they found the *Queen Anne's Revenge*." He pointed toward the ocean side of the island. "Right off the tip of this island."

"Blackbeard's ship, right?" Diana said.

"Yeah." Then Jeremy asked, "So since you love animals so much, are you planning to be a veterinarian or something?" Jeremy asked.

Diana blushed. "Stephanie and I helped a veterinarian do surgery once on a wolf-dog. That was really cool, wasn't it, Steph?"

I had been terrified. "Sure," I said.

"The vet said the animals of the world could use more people like me," Diana said. "I've never forgotten that."

"You should do it," Jeremy said. "But keep an eye on your grades. I've heard it's hard to get into vet school."

Diana opened her mouth to say something, glanced at me, and then didn't say anything. I knew exactly what she was thinking about. Being suspended. And she didn't want Jeremy to know. Well, I wasn't going to tell him if she wasn't.

I looked at the time on my phone again. "Hey, Diana, we have to go!"

"No, we don't. If they have to wait a few minutes, it's not the end of the world."

"Jeremy, how long does it take to get back to Beaufort from here?" I asked.

"About fifteen minutes."

"See, we better go. It will take time to tie up the boat and walk back to the parking lot. We're supposed to meet them in thirty minutes."

"Just a few more minutes!" Diana kept walking after the horses. I could feel myself starting to become upset. At the same time, I hardly knew Jeremy, and I didn't want to get in a fight with Diana in front of him.

"They'll get worried about us."

Now Diana wasn't even talking to me. She was just walking, ignoring me. My heart beat harder, and I felt out of breath. I could feel the blood pounding behind my eyes as I got madder and madder. Diana was always doing whatever she wanted and not paying attention to other people.

I was tired of her pushing me around.

"Diana!" I yelled, so loud that it hurt my throat, so loud that the horses started to run, crashing through the undergrowth around the trees. The pounding of their hooves gradually died away. A few branches swayed gently from their passing.

Diana threw her hands in the air in disgust. "I can't believe you did that! You scared them!"

"We have to go!" I yelled. "Why are you like this? Grammy is waiting in the hospital for us to come visit her. She's been waiting there all day!"

"I don't care!" Diana flung back over her shoulder.

Anger flashed through me. She never cares! She never cares about anyone! I ran after her, shouting. "Once I told Colleen that you cared more about animals than you did about people, and it's true!" I drew a deep breath into my lungs, feeling the burn of the cold air. And it came out. "That's why people call you 'annn-i-mal,' Diana!"

Diana stopped and turned and stared at me. "What?"

There was a sudden silence, during which the constant roar of the surf on the other side of the island seemed to swell to a crescendo inside my head. I realized that I had just told Diana the secret that I had been keeping all of this time. That I was the one who had started people calling her "animal." That it was my fault that she had endured this name-calling for over a year.

Her mouth hung open, but she seemed unable to speak. She just stared at me in shock. I stared back at her, my heart beating in my throat.

Jeremy looked from one of us to the other, then jammed his hands into his pockets and focused on the ground, scuffing the sand beneath his feet. "I guess we better go," he said finally.

In silence, we trudged back toward the meadow. Diana stayed as far away from me as she could. She and Jeremy didn't talk anymore. The wind blew and the waves pounded on the beach-side of the island with an endlessness that made me want to put my hands over my ears.

Why had I told her? Why hadn't I told her before? Would she ever understand that I hadn't done it on purpose?

15

DIANA

I walked along the sand blindly. There was a buzzing in my head, and I couldn't get my thoughts straight. I tried to remember what Dr. Shrink had told me about taking deep breaths and the Moronic Mood-O-Meter, but I felt so confused I couldn't focus on a number. How could Stephanie have done that to me? I just felt totally, totally betrayed.

The winter wind was freezing on my face and ears. I jammed my cold hands into my coat pockets. I hadn't even said good-bye to the horses.

All those people calling me names for over a year, and it was because of Stephanie? Stephanie started it? Stephanie, who, after all these months, I had finally started to trust? Stephanie, who I thought cared about me?

I felt numb.

I stumbled through the meadow and onto the sand, confused. I couldn't even look at her. I sneaked a glance at Jeremy. What must he think?

But he was standing beside the water with his hands hanging limply at his sides. He turned to me with a look of anguish on his face.

And then I looked out at the water and saw it. The tide had come in. Our boat was floating away.

It was about twenty yards out, bobbing up and down on the water. It seemed to be slipping farther away with every second.

"I forgot to drop anchor," Jeremy said.

Of course Stephanie freaked out. She gasped, tightly wrapping her arms around her body. "Oh, my gosh, what are we going to do?"

With a groaning growl of fury, Jeremy picked up a shell, and threw it at the boat. It flew over and disappeared into the water.

Then we all three stood in silence, staring at the bobbing boat. Seconds ticked by at a crawl. My thoughts raced.

"We have to do something quick!" I said. "One of us has to swim in after it!"

Stephanie looked at Jeremy with terror on her face. He drew a deep breath, took off his coat, threw it on the sand, and ran splashing into the surf, yelling at the shock of the cold water.

He waded as deep as he could, then started to swim. I ran over and picked up his coat, shouting encouragement at him. "Go, Jeremy! You can do it!"

He looked small as he stroked his way toward the boat, his reddish curls turning dark and wet. As he got closer the bow raised up and crashed down, and he dodged away, angling toward the back. Then he disappeared behind the boat. For long seconds I held my breath, waiting for him to reappear.

"Where is he?" Stephanie asked. I didn't answer.

At last I saw his head pop up over the stern, and he pulled himself, dripping, over the edge and dropped into the boat. I could only imagine how freezing he must be. He stumbled to the steering wheel and struggled with the key. It seemed to be taking him forever to start the boat. Then I realized he was shivering so violently he was having a hard time getting the key into the ignition.

"I'm sh-shaking too hard," he yelled. And then he threw a rope toward us. I ran in ankle deep and grabbed it. "Pull me in," he yelled.

I pulled as hard as I could, running up the beach, until the boat sluggishly moved into shallower water the way it had been before.

"Get in!" he called. The boat was still in a few inches of water.

I waded in, gritting my teeth against the shock of the cold water. I threw Jeremy's coat onto the boat and then clambered and shimmied onboard. Jeremy was shaking really hard, breathing through his teeth, and when I realized he was shaking too hard to put his coat on, I put it on for him.

While I was catching my breath, I could see Stephanie stop a moment to consider whether to get her new Christmas boots wet. She sat down on the sand and pulled them off. Disgusted, I ignored her when she tried to hand her boots up to me. She threw them in, and one of them landed in the bottom of the boat; the other landed on the seat.

With a rush of anger, I picked up both of them and threw them into the water.

"Oh no!" she cried. "Diana!" A look of horror crossed her face, and she raced after the boots into chest-deep water. She screamed when she felt how cold it was.

"What did you do that for?" Jeremy shouted at me. His hands and face were both bright red from the cold water.

"I'm paying her back!" I said. I caught his eye, and he looked quickly away from me with an expression of anger and disapproval. My heart thudded. Just minutes ago he had looked at me completely differently.

Stephanie had gotten the boots now and was half-wading, half-swimming back toward the boat. Jeremy reached over the side to grab the boots from her, tossed them on the floor of the boat, and then leaned over to grab Stephanie's red hands and pull her on board. She tumbled, with a wash of freezing water, onto the floor of the boat

"Are you okay?" he asked, touching her shoulder gently with a shaking hand.

She was gasping with the cold. "I'm-m-m freezing," she chattered. Stephanie picked up the boots and tried to pour the water out of them.

Jeremy gave me a dirty look. "Why did you ruin her boots?"

"She ruined a year of my life! It's not even a fair trade!" I yelled.

He shook his head, and then started looking through the storage compartments under the seats. Among a collection of lumpy life jackets, he found two old towels and a blanket. He wrapped one of the towels and the blanket around Stephanie and wrapped the remaining towel around himself.

Stephanie sat on the floor, crying. And shivering so hard.

I didn't care! She deserved it. She'd started everything. Just like I always thought, she was my enemy.

As I walked past Jeremy, intending to sit in the front, I saw that he was shivering to the point that he couldn't get his hands to stay on the steering wheel, and, like Stephanie, he was gasping with the cold.

"Di-Diana," he said. "D-drive."

Me? I didn't know how to drive a boat. I didn't know how to get back to the dock. But I looked at the way Jeremy was shaking, and I knew I had to do something. He handed me the keys and pointed to the ignition. He pointed at a T-shaped handle that was beside the wheel and described the way I had to move that handle forward to get the boat into gear and then get it moving forward. I took the wheel, and he pointed a shaking finger toward the mainland, just to the left of the island he had called Carrot Island, and I steered that way.

He sat in the passenger seat with the towel wrapped tightly around him, gritting his chattering teeth. His hair was slicked against his head and his lips were blue. I was the only one who was dry, the only one who wasn't freezing. And, of course, Stephanie was only wet because of me. It was my fault.

Nobody talked on the way back. Thank goodness it

was winter, and there were no other boats out here. I don't know what I would have done if a bunch of other boats came flying at me. My heart was in my throat, beating so hard I was sure it showed through my skin. I steered the boat where Jeremy pointed, careful not to go very fast. Stephanie huddled in the floor of the boat, still gasping from the cold.

We bumped over the waves as we headed back to shore, and I thought back to that summer of the wolves when I talked Stephanie into letting the wolves go. When my friend Russell, who loved the wolves, found out that I'd let them go, his attitude toward me was forever changed. He no longer considered me a friend, and he hadn't forgiven me.

It looked like Jeremy, who had liked me before, didn't consider me a friend any more either. Well, I didn't care!

But I did.

I glanced back at him, then at Stephanie, who was huddled on the floor of the boat, still crying. And at that moment I knew, in my core, the truth: Whatever Stephanie had said about me, she hadn't said it to hurt me. She hadn't done anything on purpose. That wasn't something she would ever do. I knew, because I knew her. She was the girl who had struggled with her fears to help me free the wolves. She was the girl who had convinced me to forgive Cody for hitting the horse at the Outer Banks. She was the girl who had believed, on the cruise, that Manuel was a good person, even though he had been persuaded to smuggle an iguana. She always believed the best about everyone.

"W-we're going to be late," Stephanie said through chattering teeth. "W-we need to tell Daddy and Lynn." She had her phone out but she'd gotten it wet when she went in the water. I realized I would have to make the call. And we were going to get in a ton of trouble.

But I had to concentrate on driving right now. I was headed toward the coast of Beaufort, with Carrot Island on my right-hand side and the Duke Marine Lab on my left. Waves lapped at the sides of a big research boat docked at Pivers Island at the Marine Lab.

"S-stay away from the research boat," Jeremy said.

I adjusted the wheel to move our boat farther away from the boat's bow as we drove by. I had figured out that I could move the T-handle toward me to slow the boat, and since we were approaching land, I did that.

With seagulls soaring above us, we slid by the houses along the Beaufort waterfront now, the sound of the water slapping against the shore. There, at last, was the dock.

"S-slow way down so you're hardly moving," Jeremy said. "Put the handle back into neutral. Just pull up alongside the dock. M-my dad can put it in the slip later."

I did as he said.

"C-cut the engine by turning the key, then grab that boat cleat and wrap the rope around it," he said. "But l-leave some p-play in the rope." He stood up to try to show me but was still shaking too ferociously to actually do it.

I turned the key to cut the engine, but of course the boat kept moving forward, so I raced to the side of the boat, leaned out, and grabbed the boat cleat as we slid by. The rear of the boat swung out and went all the way around until we were facing the other way, but I managed to hang onto the cleat. Then I threaded the rope from the bow through and around the cleat the way I'd seen Jeremy do it at Cape Lookout.

He had managed to grab another cleat, but his hands were shaking too much to get the rope in the stern over it, so I did it for him.

He nodded when I finished. "Okay."

I jumped out of the boat and held out my hand and pulled both Jeremy and Stephanie up onto the dock. Stephanie clutched the wet boots to her chest and wouldn't look at me. They were both still shivering so much I knew something was seriously wrong.

I took out the phone Dad had given me and pulled up Mom's number.

16

STEPHANIE

Daddy screeched up to the entrance of the emergency room. Lynn jumped out of the car, leaving the door hanging open, and ran inside.

Diana had called Lynn after she'd pulled the boat up to the dock, and five minutes later Lynn and Daddy were there to pick us up. I kept trying to tell Daddy we were sorry, but I was having trouble concentrating on anything.

I was still unable to get control over my shaking.

My fingers had been bright red before, but now they were blue.

A few minutes later, Jeremy and I were inside the emergency room, both on gurneys, wrapped in layers upon layers of warm white blankets. Fast-moving people in colorful scrubs had gotten us out of our wet clothes, wrapped us up in the blankets, stuck needles in our arms, and started IVs.

"It's saline solution," Lynn said, patting my arm. "It will warm you up."

I vaguely understood that Jeremy was in the cubicle next to me, a curtain drawn between us. Jeremy's parents rushed in, and between my confusion and drowsiness, I caught bits and pieces of the conversation they had with Daddy and Lynn.

"He did not have permission to take our boat out," his dad said. "I can't imagine what he was thinking, on a winter day like today …"

"And we've taught him to always drop anchor," said his mother. "I can't imagine where his mind was today."

A vague thought swam to the surface of my consciousness. I knew where Jeremy's mind had been. He'd been trying to impress Diana, that's where.

"Well, thank goodness they're going to be okay," Lynn said.

I started to feel drowsy then, and I think I fell asleep for a little while.

When I woke up, I had finally stopped shaking.

Daddy was standing by my bed. His face looked so worried. "How are you feeling, honey?"

"Okay," I said. My voice sounded weak.

"Wow, you gave us a scare," he said, stroking my hair back from my forehead.

I thought they would be so mad at us, but they weren't. They just seemed shaken and tremendously relieved. Diana was sitting in a chair in the corner of my cubicle, her face pale and serious.

"Are you okay?" she said.

"I guess so."

She nodded, biting her lip. I had never seen her like that before.

I couldn't keep track of the people taking care of me. My clothes, warm and dry from the dryer, appeared, and Lynn helped me put them back on and then wrapped me back in a new set of warm blankets.

A stern-looking doctor came by. Apparently he had seen me earlier, but I didn't remember. "Feeling better?" he asked.

I nodded.

"Well, I can let you go home now. But I want you to know how lucky you kids were," he said. "Swimming in water that cold can be life-threatening. You and the young man both had hypothermia. People have died swimming less than a hundred feet in cold water."

"Is Jeremy going to be okay?" I asked.

The doctor nodded. "His case was worse than yours, but fortunately, he's going to be okay too."

And then I heard a familiar voice.

"I can't believe I'm coming downstairs to visit my granddaughter in the emergency room! Pretty soon we'll have a family member on every floor of this hospital!"

Candace, the friendly nurse with short, dark hair we'd talked to on our first day wheeled Grammy into my cubicle in a wheelchair. "Look who's here," she said.

"Stephanie, what in the world were you doing, going into the ocean this time of year?" Grammy asked. She was pale and thinner than normal but seemed back to being her old self. "I know you wanted to be here for my surgery day after tomorrow, but you didn't have to get admitted to the emergency room. You could have just come to visit like other people."

I smiled, feeling a rush of love for her.

"Diana, what were you doing, letting her go swimming?" Grammy asked Diana.

Diana shrugged her shoulders silently and wrapped her arms around herself.

Grammy had Candace wheel her close to my bed, and she reached over and grasped my hand very tightly. "My dear granddaughter," she said, "you better promise never to scare us like that again."

I squeezed Grammy's hand. "I drew a picture of a shell for you."

And then we just stayed there, without talking, holding hands.

An hour later, Daddy helped me out of bed. On the way out to the car, we stopped by Jeremy's cubicle.

He was terribly pale and covered with blankets up to his neck. His parents stood on either side of his bed, his mother seeming concerned and his father looking angry.

"I hope you kids have learned your lesson," Jeremy's father said. "Jeremy is going to be grounded until spring break for this."

I knew Daddy and Lynn weren't that strict, and though we probably would be grounded, it wouldn't be for that long. I felt bad for Jeremy.

I glanced at Diana. Now the two of them wouldn't even look at each other.

"Get better," I said.

"Yeah," Diana mumbled.

Jeremy nodded forlornly.

Once we got home, Lynn fixed soup, and I fell right

back asleep. Diana and I didn't talk. I knew we needed to, because there were a lot of bad feelings between us, but I was too tired.

17

DIANA

I was sitting in Grammy's hospital room. Norm had gone to take a business call, and Grammy was sleeping. It was dark in here. And quiet, except for Grammy's even breathing.

Stephanie had still felt weak this morning, and Norm and Mom decided she should stay home. Mom stayed with her. I probably could have stayed home too, but I volunteered to come. I don't know why. I was glad Grammy was sleeping though, because I felt so guilty for throwing Stephanie's boots in the water that I couldn't think of much of anything to say to anyone. The fact that Stephanie had told everyone that her boots fell in made me feel even worse.

"Let's get some light in here!" Candace, Grammy's day nurse, burst in and opened the blinds, letting in strips of searing, bright sunshine.

"Oh, my," said Grammy, blinking.

"Really," I said, shielding my eyes.

"The doctor says your grandmother needs to get up and about," Candace said to me. "Her surgery is bright and early tomorrow morning. I bet you can walk her up the hall and back a few times, can't you? Help her get the blood flowing?"

"Sure." Could I? I looked at Grammy's IV stand. What if she fell? What would we talk about?

Candace threw back Grammy's covers and helped her swing her legs to the side of the bed. "You feeling up to a good walk today, Mrs. Verra?"

"Yes, much better," Grammy said. "If the doctor wants me to walk, then I'll walk."

"Okay, granddaughter," said Candace, "come over here and grab ahold of your grandmother's elbow."

I stood next to Grammy and took her elbow. She was a little unsteady on her feet, and she leaned against my shoulder.

"Just roll the IV along with you," Candace said.

We headed for the door.

"Looking great," Candace said. "Keep up the good work."

The hallway bustled with nurses hurrying back and forth and visitors coming and going. I guided Grammy around the people as best I could.

"Thank you, Diana," she said. "You didn't know you'd signed up for this, did you?" She chuckled, gripping her IV pole as she rolled it along.

"It makes me feel good to help," I said. It did. It kept my mind off my guilt. I wondered if I could just tell Grammy what I did and then have her tell me it was okay. Or have her tell me what I could do to make things right.

"Grammy?" I said. "What if someone has done something they feel bad about?"

She cut her eyes over at me, considering. "Well, what do you think a person has to do to stop feeling bad?"

"Ask the other person to forgive them?"

Grammy nodded. "That would be a good start." We walked a few more steps. "This person ... and this other person ... they're not anyone I know, are they?"

I hesitated. "No," I said.

"I didn't think so," Grammy said, with a smile.

After we'd walked one circle around the floor, I thought she'd want to go back in her room, but she didn't.

"Let's go around again," she said energetically. "I want the doctors to think I'm a star."

So I helped her put one foot in front of the other, and we went around two more times. I listened to her talk about Jelly. Maybe she would have rather had Stephanie there. But I told her she definitely was a star, and she seemed happy about that.

18

STEPHANIE

Grammy's surgery went beautifully, and Dr. Claiborne sent her home the following day. When Daddy escorted Grammy through the front door of her apartment, Jelly went wild. He began to dance around on his hind legs, yipping hysterically. Then he began to run around and around her in circles. Grammy was so happy to see Jelly she started to cry.

When Daddy sat her down on the couch, Jelly jumped onto her lap and licked the tears from her cheeks. I don't know why, but I started crying too. I guess I just felt so relieved to have Grammy back home and feeling well.

"How is my little boy?" Grammy said, stroking his head again and again. "How are you, Mr. Jelly? I missed you too!" She looked at him critically. "Norm, my dog has lost weight. Were you all not feeding him?"

"Yes, we fed him! He pined away for you, that's all, Mom," Daddy said. "He missed you so much he wasted away. You must admit he had a few pounds to spare."

Grammy laughed. "I suppose."

We got Grammy settled in her bed with Jelly curled at her feet. "It will still take me a couple of days to get back to being myself," she said. "Come on, Jelly. Take a nap with me."

And that was when Diana asked me if I wanted to take a walk on the beach. Neither Daddy nor Lynn had said anything about us being grounded, but we knew that was just because they were worried about Grammy and that we would talk about it eventually.

We put on our coats and headed out. The day was sunny and there wasn't much breeze, so it felt almost warm in the sun. As soon as we got on the sandy path to the beach Diana looked over at me.

I took a deep breath. Was she going to tell me how hurt she had been about me starting the teasing about her? I had been feeling so guilty about it for so long. I knew how mad and hurt she'd be when she found out, which was why I'd tried to keep it a secret. I had been afraid she would never forgive me. I tied my pink scarf a little more snugly around my neck.

"I'm sorry about your boots," Diana said. "I have some of my allowance saved up, and I can replace them."

I walked along beside her for a few steps. Two sandpipers ran ahead of us along the sand. She was apologizing!

"Okay," I said. I realized I'd been holding my breath, and I let it out.

Diana went on. "You haven't told Mom and Norm what I did." She put her hair behind her ear.

"Well, you didn't tell them what I did either." I walked along, playing with the fringe on my scarf. "I mean, when I figured out that what I'd said to Colleen was probably what caused you to be teased all that time, you can't imagine how bad I felt. I never meant for any of that to happen."

"I know," she said. "I was so mad on the boat, after you'd told me, and I lost control. But when I thought about it, I knew you hadn't done it on purpose."

We walked along side by side for a few minutes. The sandpipers ran to the water's edge, plunged their sharp little beaks into the wet sand looking for tiny sea creatures, and then hurried away.

"I was so scared when we had to take you and Jeremy to the hospital," Diana said. "And I kept thinking that it was all my fault that you had gotten in the water."

"I forgive you for throwing my boots in the water," I said.

Diana walked along for a short distance without answering. She was looking at the shells, then she finally stopped and picked one up, one shaped like a little whistle with a smooth ivory surface. "Would this shell be good for your collection?"

She held it out to me. She didn't have to say that she forgave me for starting the teasing. But I knew that she had.

"Oh, I wanted to find one to give Grammy. That looks perfect." And I took it and put it in my coat pocket.

I thought back to the time when Daddy and Lynn first got married and how hard it had been for Diana and me to talk to each other. I thought about how hard it had been for me to break through her anger. And now. We had our differences, but we still talked. We'd apologized to each other. We'd even forgiven each other. It seemed like a miracle. She had changed, and so had I.

Somehow, going through all those hard times made getting along the way we were now even more precious. It was something we'd fought for.

The tide was coming in, and I looked out at the grayish-green ocean and saw some surfers in wetsuits riding their surfboards.

"Look," I said to Diana.

"Oh, it's the same guys who helped me with Nick the first time he got stranded," Diana said. She waved. The surfers waved back.

The thought of Nick made us quiet for a while.

"I don't want Nick to have died for nothing," Diana went on. "I want to do something."

"Like what?"

"I don't know. I'll have to think about it."

The day Grammy came home was New Year's Eve. We tried to stay up to watch *New Year's Rockin' Eve*, but Grammy and I both fell asleep on the couch with Jelly before the ball dropped. We left to drive back to Charlotte New Year's Day, because neither Lynn nor Daddy could take any more time off work. Daddy helped Grammy hire a woman to come and take care of her until she got her strength back.

Out on Grammy's front porch, Grammy's frame felt small and bird-like as I wrapped my arms around her to say good-bye. Her cheek, when I kissed it, was soft and wrinkled. Jelly sat at her feet.

"You take care of yourself, Grammy," I said. My throat felt full, thinking about how worried we had been about her. "I hate to have to leave."

"Don't you worry. I'm going to be just fine," she said. "And maybe you'll come back and see me in the spring or summer."

Diana stepped forward, shyly, and put her arms around Grammy.

"I'm sorry I couldn't take care of Jelly for you," she said. "I'm glad you're better."

"Me too. And don't worry about Jelly. Who knows what's going on in that little mind of his."

Then Lynn hugged her tightly, and Daddy hugged her last of all. "You look great, Mom. You won't miss that gallbladder at all."

"Right," said Grammy.

Daddy didn't think anyone saw, but I did. He blinked away a tear.

As we were driving out of Grammy's neighborhood, we got a last glimpse of the emerald ocean just over the dunes.

And I thought again about whether God had answered my prayer. And I thought that maybe he had.

In the car on the way home, I got a text from Mama. Matt was still in the hospital, getting physical therapy. He was bored and in pain. Most of his college friends had gone skiing for New Year's and hadn't visited him.

When I read Mama's text, I sighed.

"What's wrong?" Diana said.

I told her.

"I'll go with you to visit him," she said. "We could take a deck of cards or something."

"You're kidding. You'd go with me?" I said.

Diana shrugged and then grinned. "Don't make me think about it too much, or I'll change my mind."

So while Lynn and Daddy were at work the next day, Mama took Diana and me to the hospital. She dropped us off so she could run errands. My heart beat really hard when I thought about seeing him.

"I'm nervous," I told Diana while we were in the elevator.

"Okay. I'll go in first," she said. We hesitantly stood in the doorway of his room. He was as pale as a ghost, without much more color in his face than the hospital gown he had on, and so thin I barely recognized him. He used to have longish brown hair. Now hair stubble, which had been shaved around the stitches in his head, was barely starting to grow back. My shock at how awful he looked must have shown on my face.

"What can I say? The food here stinks," he said.

"Yeah, I bet it does," I said. I kind of stood in the doorway and then slowly took a few steps in. "How are you feeling?"

"Like crap."

"Yeah, I can imagine." My mind raced. What else could I say to him? Mama had said she'd pick us up in forty-five minutes. What were we going to do with all that time? Right now it seemed like a million years. I noticed he had some kind of brace on his hand.

"Does that hurt?"

"Yeah. Like a bear. But I'm getting movement back."

"Oh, that's great."

"Yeah. I guess I'm lucky," he said sarcastically.

I didn't know what to say next. I grabbed a lock of my hair and twirled it.

"You are lucky. Lucky to be alive," Diana said.

Matt stared at her. "Thanks for the keen observation. I heard you got suspended from school."

"Yeah."

"You're a troublemaker. I like that."

Diana opened her mouth to answer, then seemed to reconsider. "Well, I'm turning over a new leaf," she said.

"Oh, too bad," Matt said.

"So far it's working for me," Diana said.

"Really?"

"Really."

Matt sighed and looked out the window at the hospital parking lot.

"So … you know how to play hearts?" Diana said.

"Yeah."

"Wanna play? We can help you with the cards."

Matt shrugged his shoulders, then grimaced in pain. "I guess I got nothing better to do."

Diana and I pulled the two chairs in his room close to his bed. On the blanket, Diana started dealing cards for hearts. Then she picked up his cards for him, without looking at them, and propped them in his good hand.

"I've got a good hand, get it? Ha ha," Matt said.

I was so glad she was there.

19

DIANA

It was definitely weird when Stephanie went back to school after Christmas vacation and I didn't. Mom came into my room before work that first day.

"Hey, since you've got so much time on your hands, I'm putting you to work," she said, sitting down on the end of my bed and squeezing my feet through the covers. "You can be in charge of cleaning the upstairs this week. And how about fixing dinner for the rest of us for the next couple of nights? It doesn't have to be fancy."

It wasn't. The first night I made spaghetti and bread and salad. But you'd have thought I'd made a gourmet feast the way everyone in the family raved over it.

Still, even with the extra chores, I had a lot of time to think about stuff, lying on my bed and staring at the horse posters on the wall of my room or at the bare oak trees outside my window. I kept having this dream where I'd throw Stephanie's boots in the water, and she'd jump in and the cold water would close over her head.

And I went to see Dr. Shrink.

> Me: So Stephanie was the one who started the rumors about me.
>
> Dr. Shrink: And how does that make you feel?
>
> Me: She didn't do it on purpose. I know that. But she could have died, because I threw her boots in the water. And I did do that on purpose.
>
> Dr. Shrink: So you blame yourself for that.
>
> Me: Yes, but she told Mom and Norm that her boots fell in. She didn't tell them I threw them.
>
> Dr. Shrink: How do you feel about all of that?
>
> Me: Well, we forgave each other. It's kind of a miracle that she and Jeremy ended up being okay. In fact, it's kind of a miracle that everyone ended up being okay. Matt, Stephanie's stepbrother, got drunk and crashed his car. He could have died, but he didn't. Grammy got pancreatitis, and she could have died, but she didn't. But then

Nick, that young pilot whale, ate a plastic bag he thought was a squid. And he did die.

Dr. Shrink: You've had a lot of brushes with death recently.

Me: I'm trying to make sense of it. When I think about throwing Stephanie's boots in the water, I cringe. If anything had happened to her, I would never be able to forgive myself. I have these dreams where I'm reliving that couple of seconds where I was so mad again and again. But Stephanie is okay. It's like a miracle. I want to do something.

Dr. Shrink: What do you mean?

Me: Well, I just … I just want to make a difference, in a good way. I went with Stephanie to visit Matt because she was scared, and I think I helped her. That made me feel good. And … I don't want Nick to have died for nothing. Jeremy was telling me that he planned to study marine biology. I thought it was cool the way he was so fired up about it. And I was thinking maybe I'd like to be a vet. A vet once told me the animals of the world could use my help. So I think I'm going to make that my goal.

Dr. Shrink: What does having a goal like that mean?

Me: Well, a lot of things. Study harder. Get along better with people.

Dr. Shrink: You're making great progress, Diana.

While I was suspended, I went to the barn twice. Both days Josie picked me up first thing in the morning, so I got there early enough to break the ice on the outdoor water troughs. Commanche had missed me. The first day I got back, he nuzzled my arm and made soft nickering sounds, then butted me with his head. It was comforting just to be near him.

While I was standing outside Commanche's stall, Dad called me on my new cell phone.

"Hey, dudette," he said cheerfully, as though we had never had that big fight about me coming to visit. "There's something I feel I need to tell you."

"What's that?"

"I just … well, I understand how it feels to be suspended. In fact, I got suspended once myself. For fighting."

"You did?" I caught my breath in a gasp of surprise.

"Yeah. Some guy called me something, and I turned around and punched him. I can't even remember what he called me now. I think I got mad at you, because what you did reminded me of myself. And I wasn't proud of what I did that day. And I guess I wanted to warn you about it."

As Dad was talking, I felt goose bumps prickle my neck between my shoulder blades. "Oh."

"It took me a long time to learn from my mistakes. Don't let it take so long with you. I don't mean to be impatient with you. Go back to school and turn over a new leaf. And let's plan a visit over spring break where you can do some riding, okay, dudette?"

Commanche stuck his head over the half-door and nuzzled the tip of my ear, slobbering on my phone. "Okay," I said.

That afternoon, Mom had to work late, and Norm came to pick me up. As I climbed into the car, I saw he was on the phone.

"That's great that you're making such a good recovery, Mom." He listened. "So Jelly doesn't leave your side, huh? He's happy to have you home, and we are too. Okay, talk to you soon."

I thought about how I'd acted when we were on our way to see Grammy, and I felt ashamed. Grammy didn't have to love me, but she did anyway.

But I didn't know how to tell Norm I was sorry.

"That's good that Grammy is doing well," I said. I played with the window opener, opening it and letting the cold air come in, then closing it.

Norm raised his eyebrows, as if he understood me. "Yeah, she's really lucky. And I think it meant a lot to her for us to be there with her."

He met my eyes, then patted my knee, smiling. And I knew he had forgiven me, that I didn't have to say I was sorry, that he understood.

Just like she promised, Stephanie brought me my assignments. In English, we were supposed to start our extra reading for second semester, and she brought me my book.

"We had to pick from a few different ones," she said, sitting on the end of my bed. "For me, I picked *Great Expectations* by Charles Dickens. For you, I picked *The Yearling* by Marjorie Kinnan Rawlings. It's about a boy who raises a fawn as a pet. I thought you'd like that one," she said.

I took the book, examining the picture on the front, which showed a country boy sitting in the firelight, a spotted fawn curled in his lap. I *would* like this one. It was the perfect book to pick for me.

"Thanks, Steph."

And I started thinking, maybe this is the way it should be. That Mom and Norm should meet each other and get married. That Stephanie and I could be there for each other. While we'd been at Emerald Isle, we'd watched the winter tides bring Nick ashore to die, and they'd also floated our boat away. Life, like the tides, goes on. More things in life, both good and bad, would happen to Stephanie and me. There would be times we would understand each other and there would be times we wouldn't. And it was up to us to make it mean something. And to help each other.

And I thought about the tides, the way they came in and went out, according to their own schedule, regardless of anything people did or didn't do. I realized that I had made a decision about nature and God. It was ironic, because seeing Nick die like that had made me think that there might be a God. And it had to do with the love people show each other. God is like the tides. His power is always there.

The day I went back to school, I was standing by my locker, getting ready to go to English class. I was holding the *Yearling* book Stephanie had picked for me, and Carla walked by. My heart thudded, and I felt a jolt of anger. Then I took a deep breath and began to count. The bruise on her cheek from the book I'd thrown was gone. She'd gotten her hair cut, so she had made some changes too. She glanced at me, opened her mouth to say something, then closed it. I remembered our scuffle in the hallway, the way we'd screamed at each other, the way we'd yanked at each other's clothes and clawed at each other's faces.

Then I took another deep breath, shut my locker, and turned to face her.

"Hi," I said. I gave her a smile, then I walked away.

I saw Noah in Spanish class. I started to ignore him,

the way I used to. Then I changed my mind. "Stephanie told me your grandfather was sick," I said. "How's he doing?"

Noah gave me a surprised look, then nodded. "Okay," he said. "Thanks for asking."

That night I dreamed about Nick and about the power of the tides. I dreamed that the tide had come in and gently picked him up from where he lay on the sand and floated him, light as a feather, out to sea where the other whales were waiting and calling to him with their piercing, yearning voices. And once they had Nick in their midst again, they dove deep and, together, swam for home.

Discussion Questions
for Winter's Tide

1. What do you think about both Diana and Carla getting suspended for their fight? Can you think of any situations in your own school that are similar to what happened?

2. Do you agree with Norm and Lynn's decision not to make Diana go to church? Why or why not?

3. Do you think Stephanie should tell her parents about the things Matt says to her? Do you know anyone who has had a similar experience with a stepbrother or sister?

4. Do you agree with Stephanie's mom buying her gift for Matt for her? Why or why not?

5. Why do you think Diana thinks that she hates her dad? Does she really hate him? Why or why not?

6. Are Norm and Lynn right to make Diana visit Grammy in the hospital? Do you know anyone who has had a similar experience with a family member in the hospital?

7. When Stephanie gets mad at Diana for her attitude about Grammy's illness, it's the first time she really expresses her anger to Diana. Do you agree with Stephanie? Do you think she should express her anger?

8. What did Diana and Stephanie learn about whales stranding themselves on the beach?

9. How do you think Stephanie and Diana might disagree about whether God answered Stephanie's prayer to save Grammy?

10. What are the ways in which both Diana and Stephanie change by the end of the book?

11. Do you think Jeremy's parents should have grounded him for such a long time for what he did?

12. What do you think Stephanie and Diana learn in this book about forgiveness?

Acknowledgments for Winter's Tide

For sharing their expertise on whale strandings, I would like to thank Dr. William McLellan and Dr. Ann Pabst of UNC-Wilmington's Department of Marine Biology. They so generously took time to answer my questions about what can cause whale strandings, and how the Marine Mammal Stranding Network operates when called out to a site. I would also like to thank Dr. Ari Friedlaender of the Duke University Marine Lab for answering my questions about whale behavior.

And once again, I'd like to thank...

...my writing buddy and dear friend Chris Woodworth for her keen insights and ideas. By now she knows the characters as well as I do!

...my dear friend Ann Campanella and her astute and delightful daughter Sydney. Their gentle suggestions helped make me aware of times when a young reader might look for an exploration of faith.

...my exuberant friend Deb Waldron who got updated on Stephanie and Diana each day on our walks whether she wanted to or not.

...Liz Hatley, for her kind and thoughtful comments.

…Caryn Wiseman, my agent, whose support has been so key.

…Kim Childress, my editor, for her wise suggestions and her faith in my work, which means so very much to me. Many people at Zondervan have worked to support this series, and I deeply appreciate all that they have done.

…and most of all, my husband, children, parents, and brother—for their steadfast love.